MONTANA MAVERICKS

Welcome to Big Sky Country! Where spirited men and women discover love on the range.

THE TRAIL TO TENACITY

Tenacity is the town that time forgot, home of down-to-earth cowboys who'd give you the (denim) shirt off their back. Through the toughest times, they've held their heads high, and they've never lost hope. Take a ride out this way and get to know the neighbors—you might even meet the maverick of your dreams!

Marisa Sanchez is not about to be swayed by a rich cowboy, no matter how smooth-talking or good-looking. She's a sensible woman who is sure she's immune to Dawson John's charms. But after catching a glimpse of the real man behind his confident swagger, she starts second-guessing herself. Should she do what's safe? Or follow her heart?

Dear Reader,

Thank you for choosing Dawson John and Marisa Sanchez's opposites-attract romance just in time for the holidays!

Dawson John is a handsome, wealthy rancher born into a powerful family in Bronco, Montana. When it comes to women, he's looking for fun, not forever. Until sassy Marisa Sanchez waltzes into his life and Cupid's arrow with her name on it pierces his heart. How can he convince her that he is husband material? For the first time, Dawson can't get what he wants with a wink and a smile.

Marisa Sanchez is a music teacher from a barely blue-collar family in Tenacity, Montana. When a video of her multicultural approach to the previous year's Tenacity holiday show goes viral on TikTok, Marisa is offered a job producing the Mistletoe Pageant in the neighboring town of Bronco. And this is where her life unexpectedly collides with swoon-worthy Dawson John. Marisa has always dreamed of a humble, hardworking Tenacity man dedicated to community service for her husband. A devil-may-care cowboy like Dawson did *not* fit that bill!

Will Dawson and Marisa's holiday fling be little more than a shooting star streaking across the Montana night sky: white-hot and gone too soon? Or will Dawson and Marisa find a way to bridge their differences and forge a love that will last them a lifetime?

My best always,

JoAnna Sims

PS: My website, joannasimsromance.love, is under construction. Watch this space!

THE MAVERICK'S CHRISTMAS KISS

JoAnna Sims

MONTANA MAVERICKS

Special thanks and acknowledgment are given to JoAnna Sims for her contribution to the Montana Mavericks: The Trail to Tenacity miniseries.

MONTANA MAVERICKS

Recycling programs for this product may not exist in your area.

ISBN-13: 978-1-335-14315-0

The Maverick's Christmas Kiss

Harlequin Enterprises ULC
22 Adelaide St. West, 41st Floor
Toronto, Ontario M5H 4E3, Canada
www.Harlequin.com

Printed in Lithuania

MIX
Paper | Supporting responsible forestry
FSC® C021394

JoAnna Sims is proud to pen contemporary romance for Harlequin Special Edition. JoAnna's series The Brands of Montana features hardworking characters with hometown values. You are cordially invited to join the Brands of Montana as they wrangle their own happily-ever-afters.

Books by JoAnna Sims

Montana Mavericks: The Trail to Tenacity

The Maverick's Christmas Kiss

Harlequin Special Edition

The Brands of Montana

A Match Made in Montana
High Country Christmas
High Country Baby
Meet Me at the Chapel
Thankful for You
A Wedding to Remember
A Bride for Liam Brand
High Country Cowgirl
The Sergeant's Christmas Mission
Her Second Forever
His Christmas Eve Homecoming
She Dreamed of a Cowboy
The Marine's Christmas Wish
Her Outback Rancher
Big Sky Cowboy
Big Sky Christmas

Montana Mavericks: Six Brides for Six Brothers

The Maverick's Wedding Wager

Visit the Author Profile page
at Harlequin.com for more titles.

Dedicated to Jacqueline Sumner-Davis

Thank you for being the sister I always wanted.

You are brilliant, beautiful and as tough as tungsten steel.

I love you and I am so grateful to have you in my life.

Your Big Sis

Prologue

Tenacity Elementary School
Tenacity, Montana
December 2006

It was two weeks until Christmas Eve, and eight-year-old Marisa Sanchez had just performed in the Tenacity Elementary holiday show. Like many of her peers, she had auditioned for the holiday show, but only she had won the coveted spot of the star on top of the singing Christmas tree. Her mother was a seamstress by trade and, with materials that she had been provided by the school, she had designed and sewn the costumes.

Dressed as a puffy, bright yellow five-point star with a small hole in the top point for her face, Marisa was now standing in line to greet the music teacher, Mrs. Jankowski, who had produced the holiday show. Her parents and her brothers, Julian, Diego and Luca, along with her sister, Nina, stood beside her. Marisa's face was flushed and her dark brown eyes were shining from her triumphant performance. Yes, it was difficult for her to wait, but the wait was totally worth it to spend a moment with her favorite teacher.

Before taking her turn with her teacher, Marisa tugged on her mother's hand to get her attention.

Her mother leaned down and asked, "Yes, *mija*?"

"Remember how scared I was?"

"I do," her mother said.

"Guess what?"

"What?"

Marisa smiled up at her mother. "Once I got onstage, I wasn't scared anymore. I was the very best Christmas star I could be."

This made her mother laugh. "Yes, you were, *mija*. A perfect Christmas star!"

When it was *finally* their turn, Marisa threw herself into Mrs. Jankowski's arms and hugged her tightly.

"My beautiful little star!" The music teacher returned her hug. "You were the perfect topper for our Christmas tree!"

"Thank you, Mrs. Jankowski," Marisa said with a happy grin.

"You are welcome, precious one." Mrs. Jankowski gave her one last big squeeze before she turned her attention to Marisa's parents, shaking hands first with her father and then her mother.

"Mr. and Mrs. Sanchez, thank you so much for coming," the music teacher exclaimed. "I hope you all enjoyed the show."

"We loved the show," Nicole said. "We didn't know that Marisa could sing just like a pretty little songbird."

That made Mrs. Jankowski's smile broaden. "Your daughter is very talented. She has a beautiful voice and she is picking up the piano so quickly."

"Thank you so much for everything you have done for our daughter," Will said while Marisa basked happily in the praise of her teacher.

"Of course!" the teacher said with a nod before she

added, "And thank you, Mrs. Sanchez, for making our costumes. The Kindergarten Christmas show never looked so good!"

"I was so pleased to be able to help," Nicole said, putting her arm around Marisa the Five-pointed Star.

"Well," Will said, glancing at the parents and students waiting to greet the teacher. "We'd better let you go."

As her family moved on, Mrs. Jankowski had one final had one final word for her parents. "Please consider getting music lessons for Marisa. I would start with voice and piano, as she is really quite gifted."

Marisa waved goodbye to her teacher as she walked with her family to the parking lot. As expected, the older siblings held the hands of their younger siblings, and because it was her special night, Marisa walked between her parents holding their hands and swinging every couple of feet. Marisa was feeling so happy, but there was something bothering her. When Mrs. Jankowski had mentioned lessons, a dark cloud of worry had passed over her parents' faces. Their house was full of love and family and laughter, but money was always tight. Even at her tender age, Marisa was aware that, even though they were rich in the love department, they were considered poor when it came to money. Many times when she asked for something that she saw other kids in school had, her mother, with a deep sadness in her eyes, would tell her that they would have to wait. Her father worked on a ranch and rented land to farm, growing hay for the animals. Will also regularly took on odd jobs to make ends meet while her mother sewed nearly seven days a week.

Once their family of seven was seated in her father's van, her mother met her husband's eyes. "Lessons. Can we manage that?"

Will was silent for several seconds, then he broke the gaze with his wife and stared out of the windshield that had a small crack in the center, his hands gripping the steering wheel so tightly that his knuckles had blanched white.

"We will figure it out, my love," her father said. "Somehow, someway, we will get our sweet angel those lessons. You heard her teacher—she is talented."

"I can take on more sewing," her mother said with a nod and a look of determination on her face.

"And I can take on more handyman jobs," her father agreed, his jaw set.

"She can have our mowing money," Julian said, and her brothers Diego and Luca nodded their agreement.

Will Sanchez looked back at his boys. "Thank you. You make us so proud."

Little Nina piped up and said, "Marisa can have my birthday money."

"My lovely Nina," her mother said, "you are such a sweet thing."

"Wait a minute! Am I going to take music lessons?" Marisa asked, her eyes, wide with hope, dancing between her parents' faces.

Her mother smiled at her. "We will have to see what Santa left under the Christmas tree for you."

Chapter One

Twenty-six-year-old music teacher Marisa Sanchez peeked out from behind the stage curtain at Bronco Theater to see how many folks answered her advertisement for open auditions to perform in the annual Mistletoe Pageant, a show full of singing, dancing and holiday cheer. A very nice crowd of potential performers were seated in the curved rows of the theater. Relieved, Marisa let go of the curtain with an excited smile on her face. She loved a challenge and the town of Bronco had certainly given her one: she had been hired to organize and direct the annual Mistletoe Pageant.

Marisa took one more quick scan of the crowd and that was when her eyes zeroed in on a dusty-haired cowboy finding a seat in the back row of the theater. He wore casual western clothing that had an exacting fit across his broad shoulders and tall, muscular frame. The quality of his clothing, along with his confident swagger, screamed "money" and "privilege," which was always a turnoff for her. His companion was a willowy, leggy blonde with a face meant for modeling. That cliché made Marisa dismiss the cowboy as shallow and self-important.

"Marisa?"

At the sound of a voice behind her, Marisa startled and

spun away from the curtain as if she had been caught in the act of doing something wrong.

"Yes, Agnes?"

Agnes Little, her "go-to" person at the Bronco Theater, was a dear woman in her late sixties who had worked at the theater for decades.

"Would you like to get started?" Agnes asked. "It's six minutes past one."

"Yes. Thank you so much for keeping me on schedule."

"My pleasure." Agnes beamed at her. "If you stand right there on that mark, I will open the curtain for you."

Marisa took her spot on the mark, closed her eyes, took in a deep breath and knew that once the curtain opened, those pesky nerves would evaporate. Agnes walked over to the thick cord that would allow her to manually pull open the heavy maroon curtain.

"Ready?" Agnes asked.

She was ninety percent ready and ten percent slightly nauseous. Her norm.

After one quick silent prayer, Marisa opened her eyes, chin up, shoulders back, and said to Agnes, "Let's get this party started."

"Dawson!" Charity put her hand on his arm and shook it. "That's her!"

Dawson John wanted to focus on his phone while mentally willing time to pass at warp speed so he could get out of this musty, old relic of a theater and once again breathe in the fresh Montana air.

All he had done was offer Charity a lift to her audition because her truck was in the shop; he had planned on dropping her off and picking her up after it was over. But then

Charity, as usual, had to go and complicate it. Now she wanted him to stay for moral support.

"No good deed goes unpunished," he muttered as he sent a text then slipped his phone into the front pocket of his designer button-down shirt.

Charity had turned around so she could take a selfie with the woman on the stage in it. And for some unfathomable reason, Charity had the exact expression on her face as when she had gotten her first Range Rover.

"Are you okay?" he asked her.

"I am." Charity pointed to the stage. "That's Marisa Sanchez! I'm a total fan girl. I can't believe she's actually here!"

"Who the heck is Marisa Sanchez?" he asked, feeling an odd combination of irritation and curiosity.

"For us theater geeks, she's kind of a big deal right now. One of her videos went viral on TikTok," Charity explained.

Dawson turned his attention from his phone to take a good look at the amazing Marisa Sanchez. There, standing alone and poised at center stage, was a woman who looked to be around Charity's age—maybe a bit older. She was rather short—he liked his women tall. She had straight long hair as glossy as a raven's wing. He had always preferred blondes. She had a curvy hourglass figure, and while some guys were into that, he favored women with an athletic build. Women who could keep up with him when he rock climbed, white water rafted or BASE-jumped. The wondrous Marisa Sanchez looked more like the type to curl up on the couch with a good book. After a quick appraisal of her, Dawson could not fathom why these artsy folks in the theater were acting as if they had just found Elvis alive in Bronco Theater.

His phone rang, and he was happy for the excuse to exit stage left.

Charity managed to take her eyes off her idol for a second to ask him, "Where are you going?"

He held out the phone for her to see. "I have to take this."

"Okay." Charity frowned at him. "Promise you'll be back in time for my audition."

He made a cross over his heart and winked at her, then he answered the phone while he headed out to the lobby.

"Natasha," Dawson said with a pleased smile, "how did you know I needed to be rescued?"

"Now why would a strapping cowboy like you need to be rescued by little ole me?"

"You'd be surprised."

"Maybe I would," the woman on the other end of the line said. "Maybe I wouldn't."

Dawson had eaten the night before at The Association, a private dining club for wealthy ranchers where the John family had a long-standing membership. Besides appreciating the excellent food, spirits and backroom deals at the club, Dawson loved catching the eye of the beautiful women employed there. It was a perfect scenario—most of the women were just passing through on their way to find a bigger and better life outside of Montana. Romancing women with an expiration date was zero risk and all reward for him. Simple. Clean. No fuss, no muss. Last night, he had met a sexy redheaded bartender named Natasha, and he was eager to make her time in Bronco memorable.

"Are you willing to take my word for it?" he asked flirtatiously.

"Not a chance. I gave up trusting cowboys like you a long while back."

"Been burnt?"

"Plenty."

"I guess I bet on the wrong horse." Dawson frowned. It felt odd to be rejected.

"Now, Dawson." Natasha's voice turned silky and sensual. "Don't go hurting my feelings by giving up so easily."

"You're beautiful and you know it."

"The same could be said of you."

Dawson went quiet while he conducted a cost-benefit analysis. Perhaps Natasha was turning out to be way more of headache than he was looking for.

After a short silence between them, the bartender said, "I'd be happy to take you out for a nice, long ride if that's all you're after."

"No attachments?"

"None whatsoever."

"Is there a secret password to this nirvana of which you speak? *Open sesame*?"

That made Natasha laugh and he liked the sound of it. "Offer me a nightcap, Dawson. The rest will come easy between us or it won't."

"Lovely. Natasha, would you like to have a nightcap with me?"

"Pick me up after my shift. Eleven o'clock sharp. I don't wait."

"Neither do I."

Marisa had stood on the stage looking out at the people who were there to audition. There were moms and dads with their children, and that brought up so many emotions tied to her childhood in school plays and at the community theater. These experiences had quite literally brought her to this moment in her life. She also saw some folks standing for her and clapping *very* enthusiastically while simultaneously filming her on their phones. She imagined that these might just be some of her TikTok fans, which was still an odd concept for her to get her head around.

"Thank you so much, Bronco!" Marisa smiled broadly and clapped her hands for them. "It is my pleasure to be here with you. Thank you for coming. Let's make this the best darn Mistletoe Pageant that Bronco, Montana, has ever seen!"

She made sure that she looked at all sides of the theater to acknowledge everyone. For barely a moment, Marisa's eyes caught and held the gaze of the perfectly made cowboy in the back row. He didn't look away and neither did she. And then something truly unusual and notable happened: those familiar, sweet, darling butterflies turned into a giant boulder roiling around like a washing machine overloaded with towels.

The cowboy was first to break eye contact and then he got up and left the theater. And that action made her smile falter for a second. It felt like a rejection and that irritated her and she brushed that feeling aside and refocused her attention to what was really important: musical theater auditions!

Marisa had forgotten that audition day, while at times exciting and invigorating, could also be long and exhausting. Marisa worked her way through the alphabetized list of children first and then the adults, and after she had finished the *I* names, she decided to take a fifteen-minute break.

After accepting a burnt cup of coffee from Agnes, Marisa returned to her place at the piano. She flipped the *I* page over to *J* on the adult list and called the first name on that page.

After securing a date with Natasha for the evening, Dawson took his time returning to the theater. Charity had always been involved with the arts and he wanted to support her, he really did. But sitting in a theater for an entire afternoon while listening to people butchering holiday classics? No thanks. After he strolled around town a bit, he returned to the theater and he took his seat next to Charity. She was sitting forward on her seat, her arms crossed in front of her body, and she barely glanced his way.

"What'd I miss?" he asked her in his best cajoling voice.

She didn't respond, and that's the moment he realized that he'd screwed up royally.

"Hey." He leaned over and whispered, "I'm sorry."

"Where have you been?" she whispered back, still refusing to look at him.

"Ah, heck, Charity. I hate this sort of thing. You know that."

"Yeah, I do," she replied. "But I thought you loved me enough to suffer through it."

Dawson felt like he'd been punched in the nose; the way she put it made him feel like the biggest jerk in the world.

"I do, Charity. You know I do. Have you gone yet?"

"No. Not yet."

Dawson saw Marisa glance their way and Charity saw it too.

"Shhh. We aren't supposed to be talking during someone else's performance."

Dawson's hackles went straight up and he wanted to say, in a louder voice, that it was a free country and he could do whatever he wanted to do wherever he wanted to do it. But because Charity was already pretty sore at him, he decided to follow the rules. He even clapped for the young man who had just finished his audition to show Charity that he *was* there to support her.

"Charity?" Marisa called the name. "Charity John?"

Charity stood up and he could tell by the expression on her face that she was feeling uncertain. He stood up too, gave her a bear hug and said, "You've got this, Charity. Go show Miss TikTok what *you* can do."

In her peripheral vision, Marisa had noticed the cowboy return and take a seat next to his companion. Their talking had been a distraction, and if they hadn't stopped when they did, she would have marched up the stairs and told them to knock it off. Now that Charity walked by on her way to the stage, Marisa realized the young woman was a knockout with large eyes surrounded by long, dark lashes, a petite nose, and a toothy white smile that lit up her face. She had sweetness about her that Marisa hadn't expected.

"Hello, Charity," she said. "Nice to meet you."

"It's really great to meet you, Marisa," Charity said in a breathy voice. "I love your videos."

"Thank you. The pleasure is all mine," Marisa said. "What will you be sharing with us today?"

"'Last Christmas' by Wham," Charity said shyly. "I know it's a strange choice."

Marisa took the sheet music that Charity had handed to her and flipped through the pages quickly. "I don't think it's a strange choice. I think it's an insightful choice."

This compliment earned a smile from Charity that started with her lips and ended in her eyes. "Thank you. I was so worried about it."

"Let that worry go," Marisa said. "You had a brilliant idea. Now, get up on that stage and own it."

As Dawson watched Charity onstage, he actually began to worry for her. She seemed so nervous and so young standing there that he found himself silently praying for her success. Instead of sitting down, he kept standing and gave her two thumbs-up signs, which made her smile. The moment Charity began to sing, he felt the hair on his arms stand up. It had been a while since he had heard her perform; he had no idea how beautiful her voice had become. Dawson started to clap for her, calling out encouraging words. He thought he was helping until he saw a look of horror mar Charity's face as she shook her head at him and faltered. Marisa stopped playing, stood up and marched up the aisle to him.

"Hey! Cowboy. Please don't clap or stomp your feet or whistle or yell during the audition. It is very distracting. If you can't follow my rules, I will need you to wait outside until your girlfriend has finished."

Dawson watched Marisa walk away from him before he slumped back into his seat. He could feel the disapproving gazes of the audience and the humiliation emitting from Charity. Screw up number two! But he knew he could make amends with his sister later. Right now he was too focused on the mind-altering thing that had just happened to him.

He'd been run over by a freight train named Marisa Sanchez.

Chapter Two

Dawson would need time to process this moment. All he had done was look into Marisa Sanchez's stormy, soulful brown eyes and he had experienced what he could only describe as an entire system meltdown. His heart was pounding in his chest as if he had just climbed up the peak of a high altitude mountain. He couldn't seem to take his eyes off of the woman at the piano and, in all honesty, he didn't want to.

Charity finished her song and everyone, including him, clapped enthusiastically for her. Charity sent him a sweet smile; that meant she had forgiven him. After a brief conversation with Marisa, Charity returned to their row of seats.

"You were amazing." He hugged her, then they sat down. "You're a star."

"Thank you. I really liked having you here with me."

"Except for when I interrupted your audition."

"I forgive you, of course," Charity said and then whispered, "I want to watch the rest of the auditions. I can catch a ride home. I know several people here."

"No," he said quickly. "I'll hang out and watch."

Charity looked at him with a truly surprised expression on her face. "Why would you do that?"

He tried to act nonchalant. "I know I haven't always liked things like this…"

"You loathe them."

"That's a strong word."

"An accurate word," she said quickly as the next performer's name was called. "You barely made it back in time to hear me sing!"

Dawson was about to debate her more, but Marisa looked at them both and he clammed up. He stayed even when one of the singers sounded like a bullhorn on a foggy day; he stayed even when a singer was so off-key that it hurt his ears. He stayed through every mind-numbing, ear-splitting performance. And watched Marisa.

Finally, a young man took the stage and he began to sing "Oh Come All Ye Faithful." Even Dawson could hear that his pitch was perfect and his voice filled the room taking everyone, including him, on an emotional journey. When they reached one of the quieter moments of the song, when the young man was about to take them back up to a peak, Dawson's phone rang loudly. He had turned up the volume so he could hear it over the singing before he knew he was breaking a rule. Several people around them groaned and swiveled their heads to give him a well-deserved death stare.

"Turn it off!" Charity whispered harshly to him.

"I will!" He fished inside of his shirt pocket for the phone only to recall that he had put it in the back pocket of his jeans. He stood up, grabbed the phone and fumbled to shut it down, while Marisa glared at him.

"Turn it off!" Charity said again, burying her head in her hands.

"I'm trying! Can't you see that I'm trying?"

He grabbed the phone, hit the red button to hang up,

turned off the volume, and then apologized to everyone around him; he was about to sit back down when he saw Marisa pointing at the door. Sheepishly, Dawson ducked out of the theater and stood alone in the lobby.

He looked at the door he had just walked through, puzzled. He had never believed in love at first sight. And now he was pretty sure that he was wrong about that.

He was also pretty sure, but not entirely sure, that the woman of his sudden onset affection disliked him intensely.

"Well, lookie here! Dawson John in my theater? All grown up!" Agnes gave him a tight hug before she stepped back to beam up at him from her short stature. "Are you auditioning?" Agnes Little had taught music at his elementary school. She had taught the Abernathy and Taylor kids as well as his brothers and sister. She was beloved by the parents and the children who had her for a teacher. Now, in her second act after retirement, Agnes wore as many different hats as needed to keep the doors of the community theater open for performances throughout the year, especially the annual Mistletoe Pageant.

"Me?" He winced. "Not a snowball's chance."

Hands on narrow hips, Agnes asked, "Now, you aren't still bent out of shape about the cactus incident, are you? It's not kind to hold a grudge against someone of my age."

"You told me that I was talented at standing stiffly onstage."

"Yes." She nodded. "Yes, I did. And it was true. You were very good at that and it wasn't a skill that just anyone had, so it made perfect sense to cast you as the important role of the cactus." Agnes continued, "And it would break my heart if I had ruined musical theater for you in any way."

"I'm okay," he said.

Agnes shot him a smile, pat him on the arm and said,

"I'll sleep better tonight. Now that's the God's honest truth. Good to see you. Say 'hi' to the folks. Work to be done, so I'd best shuffle off…"

"What do you know about Marisa Sanchez?"

Agnes turned around and looked at him. "Not much. She's a music teacher, so I feel a kinship with her. She cares about kids and the planet."

"She's a force." For some reason, he *needed* to tell someone, anyone, about what had just happened to him. Struck by lightning and left lovesick.

"From my limited knowledge—" she shrugged "—I think that sums her up, yes."

Dawson looked at Agnes and couldn't seem to form the thoughts in his mind into actual words.

"Dawson. I love you, my boy. Did you know that the older you are, the quicker you get old? When we started this conversation, I was sixty-seven. Now I'm knocking on the door of sixty-eight. Blink twice if you can hear me."

His next words were blurted out. "I interrupted Marisa's auditions. How do I apologize?"

Agnes shook her head, looked down at the toes of her sensible black shoes and said, "Love. It's always love, isn't it?"

"I don't know what this is," Dawson said with a confused shake of his head. "All I did was look into her eyes and then…"

"Lightheaded, heart racing out of control?"

"I feel like my heart is suddenly too big for my body like that Grinch guy." He wiped off his forehead and then looked at his hand. "I'm sweating. It's hot in here. Is it hot in here? Or is it just me?"

"It's just you."

"I don't feel well at all, Agnes." He said, "I think I need to go to a doctor."

"Well, I'm not a doctor per se, but I do have a pretty good idea what's ailing you."

He looked at her intently, awaiting her next pearls of wisdom.

"My diagnosis?" Agnes stated, "You have a classic case of love at first sight."

Dawson shook his head. "No."

"Yes."

"That can't be right. Can it?"

"I know what I know."

Dawson still felt completely perplexed, like a cartoon character that had been run over and stood up flattened.

"Then what should I do?" he asked. "I don't think she's at all fond of me and we haven't even met."

"That's a brainteaser, no doubt about it," Agnes agreed. "Can I give you a bit of advice?"

"No."

"I recommend that you say you're sorry with hot chocolate."

He furrowed his brow. "That doesn't seem like much of an apology."

Most women he'd met along the way would throw that hot chocolate in his face right before they dragged him through the mud on social media and then put the final nail in his coffin by blocking him on their phone.

"That's your absolute best advice?"

"Yes, it is," Agnes said. Then she added, "Heavy on the marshmallows." She heaved a sigh. "Well, I've got a tight schedule. Good luck to you!"

Agnes was a woman who had a keen sense about people. She was known for it. And did he really have a better idea for how to smooth over things with Marisa? No. He didn't. The apology tools in his toolbox would work with most women he knew, but not Marisa Sanchez. He'd bet money on that. It was Agnes's advice or nothing.

After the last audition ended, everyone began filing out of the theater. Marisa felt drained from the long day but also excited by the level of talent she had seen in Bronco. And even though she was ready to wind down after a hectic day, she spent time with the performers who wanted to speak with her when the auditions were done. She noticed Charity John walk toward her as the line finally began to dissipate.

"I am so sorry about the clapping and the cheering and the phone ringing," the blonde said, apologizing.

Marisa smiled a tired smile and wanted to set her mind at ease. "It's fine, Charity. No real harm done. Just maybe remind your boyfriend to turn the volume off on his phone next time."

Charity laughed. "Dawson isn't my boyfriend. He's my brother."

"So that's who he is." Marisa didn't understand it and she couldn't even find words to describe it, but knowing that the cowboy wasn't Charity's boyfriend made her feel... inexplicably happy.

Charity continued, "Honestly, you probably won't see Dawson again. He was only here today to give me a ride. My mechanic texted me earlier and said that my truck is ready."

"Oh. I see." Was that disappointment she heard in her own voice? *Odd.*

Charity continued, bringing Marisa's focus back to their conversation. "Thank you for your coaching today. It was a big help."

"You have a gift, Charity. Your voice is a gift."

A pretty blush appeared on Charity's high cheekbones. "Thank you. I'm worried that I picked up some bad habits from my time in beauty pageants. Mom started me when I was a baby." She laughed and it was a pleasant tinkling sound. "I actually have a crown from when I was one year old!"

Marisa smiled along with her. Charity was exactly the type of person Marisa enjoyed; she was kind, gentle and didn't take herself too seriously.

"Do you still participate in pageants?" Marisa asked.

Charity furrowed her brow and shook her head. "No. I broke my mom's southern belle heart, but Miss Bronco 2022 was my last."

"Well," Marisa said, "now I understand why you have so much poise onstage. You look right at home."

Charity hugged her tightly and said, "Even if I don't get a singing role, I promise I will be here to help you any way I can."

"I really appreciate that. I'm in a new town, and I could use all the support I can get."

Charity looked at her directly. "You can count on me, Marisa."

"Thank you."

The door to the theater opened and she saw the cowboy—Dawson—now she knew his name, walked through. Charity waved at him, thanked her again, and then easily took the stairs two steps at a time to reach her brother. When she reached him at the top step, Charity waved goodbye. And, as quick as a flash, Marisa met Dawson's steady gaze again. As brother and sister disappeared into the theater lobby, Marisa was left standing by the piano, temporarily frozen in her spot. Then, she felt a wave of dizziness and that made her put her hand on her stomach and sit down heavily on the piano chair.

She closed her eyes, fighting an uncomfortable woozy sensation that was followed by her heart racing so quickly that she wondered if she had developed some sort of cardiac problem.

"Miss Marisa?" Agnes found her slumped forward, her arms resting on the closed keys, her head down and resting on her folded hands. "Are you okay?"

Marisa sat up slowly. "Yes. I'm just tired. Or coming down with a bug. Or both."

"Can I get you something to eat?"

"No." Marisa shook her head, "My aunt and uncle expect me later. Is it okay if I stick around for a bit? Music always helps me clear my head."

"Well, of course you can," Agnes said. "And we can talk about the auditions tomorrow when you're not so tuckered."

"Thank you."

"You do seem a bit flushed in the cheeks. What *are* your symptoms?" Agnes asked in a no-nonsense tone. Like a detective searching for clues.

"Dizzy, I guess, and lightheaded. My heart was racing."

Agnes looked at her and after a moment said, "There seems to be a lot of that going around today."

"Really?" she asked, putting her hand on her forehead. "*Is* there a bug going around? I can't get sick now. I don't have time to be sick."

"Don't you worry about that, dear one," Agnes said. "The kind of sickness going around this theater can't be healed with medication."

After dropping Charity off at the mechanic's and making sure that the truck was back in working order, Dawson headed straight to a nearby coffee shop and ordered two large hot chocolates *with* marshmallows on the side, then drove back to the theater to hopefully catch Marisa before she left for the day. When they were on the way to the mechanic, the only subject Charity wanted to talk about was Marisa. And he didn't mind one bit. He wanted to know more about the director of the Mistletoe Pageant, so he listened carefully. Just before they arrived, Charity told him that Marisa was such a hard worker and so dedicated that she was going to be creating a new arrangement for a Christmas carol, and wasn't that amazing?

What was amazing to him was the information Charity had given him. Marisa would be at the theater, and he needed to apologize quick before her possible bad opinion of him was set in stone. Maybe it was a long shot, and maybe this was a fool's errand, but he *had* to try. And even though he felt a twinge of guilt for keeping his plan from Charity, if something came of it, she would be happy, and if it didn't, he could walk away without telling anyone about his failed attempt at winning Marisa over.

Marisa closed her eyes, felt the keys with her hands and listened to the notes with her heart. One measure at a time, she listened carefully, stringing more notes together in a way that remained true to the song "Jingle Bells."

"I've never heard 'Jingle Bells' played like that before."

Marisa's fingers froze, and she opened her eyes to find Dawson John standing a couple of feet away from her; they were the only two people left in the theater.

"I love the original arrangement, of course, but I also think that it's fun to jazz it up a bit," she said, not at all sure why he hadn't left with his sister.

"I liked it. I'm Dawson, by the way. Dawson John."

"Yes. I know." Her tone was more abrupt than she had intended. "Charity told me."

After he didn't fill in the silence, she added, her guard up, "I'm Marisa. But I think you may already know that."

Marisa *had* never "swooned." Prone. Yet, up close, Dawson John was so incredibly handsome with his tanned skin, dusty-blond hair tussled in a very sexy way, his icy-blue eyes, strong nose, perfect jawline, perfect teeth and lips that were meant for kissing, Marisa was certain she *was* on the verge of a swoon. He could easily be mistaken for a Hemsworth brother from an American mother; he looked as if he had stepped right out of magazine or onto a movie set where he, obviously, would be playing the role of leading man. Those broad shoulders, those heavily muscled arms and legs, and gosh darn it, he smelled delicious—vanilla and spices found in a pumpkin pie all rolled into one—and she was *very* hungry.

"Is there something I can do for you, Dawson?" Marisa managed to ask the question in a breathy voice that did not even remotely sound like her own.

"No. Maybe. Yes."

In that moment, he seemed more human to her, and when she laughed, and then he laughed with her, the fog of an uncomfortable awkwardness between them lifted.

Dawson held up one finger. "Wait right here."

"Okay."

Marisa watched Dawson jog up the steps, retrieve a bag and walk back to her quickly.

"Why did you hide that bag?" Marisa asked. "You don't have a knife in there, do you?"

Dawson smiled at her while he opened the bag from Bronco Java and Juice.

"No." He laughed. "What I have in here is an apology. And I hid it just in case you kicked me out again."

"Only if you ignore the rules," she countered, her curiosity officially piqued. "What's the apology for?"

"Breaking your rules." He took two cups out of the bag labeled Bronco Java and Juice.

"I don't think you need to apologize. It occurred to me that you'd missed my audition rules, and I felt bad about how I spoke to you. So, I apologize. My only excuse is that I'm super stressed out about this job."

"I couldn't tell. You looked perfectly at ease, quietly confident. Impressive, really," Dawson said. "How about I forgive you and you forgive me?"

Marisa smiled at him, and she had a gut feeling that she would remember this moment for the rest of her life. She held out her hand to shake his, and the minute their hands touched, a spark of electricity jumped between them.

"Did you feel that?" he asked her in a direct manner she liked.

Of course she had—she couldn't have missed it! "I did," she admitted, and then she did her best to redirect the conversation. "What's in the cups?"

There was that swoonworthy smile of his. "Hot chocolate. For two."

Her eyes widened in surprise. "Agnes?"

"Agnes."

"Why don't we sit down on the stage? I don't want to have anything liquid around this piano or on the floor. I want to stay on Agnes's good list."

"Ditto."

They both walked up the stairs to the stage and sat down together.

Marisa sat cross-legged, picked up her cup, held it in her

hands to enjoy its warmth and then she took a small sip of the piping hot liquid.

"Is it good?" he asked.

"It's so good," she said with a thankful smile. "I really appreciate this, Dawson. You didn't have to, but thank you."

"My pleasure. But how about I make it even better?" He pulled out a baggie of small marshmallows he had asked for on the side. He showed her the bag and she laughed.

"You have excellent intel, don't you?"

He sprinkled some marshmallows into her cup and then dropped some into his.

"I suppose I do. I've never really needed it before, but it did come in handy this time."

Marisa wasn't sure what he meant when he had said *I've never really needed it before* but didn't ask. Things were easy between them, oddly comfortable; she didn't want to rock that boat. But it did not escape her that she wasn't at all certain why Dawson John was with her right now. This was too elaborate for only an apology from her point of view. What exactly was his ulterior motive? She wanted to know, so she asked.

"Are you trying to influence my decision about Charity?"

Dawson looked at her with a frown on his perfectly symmetrical face. Could she be reading that correctly? Had there been a flash of hurt in those ocean-blue eyes?

"No," he said, "I'm not."

"Then why?"

"Why am I here?"

She nodded wordlessly.

After several silent moments and after Dawson had stared out into the empty rows of seats.

When he turned his eyes back to her face, her unexpected companion said, "I'm here because of you."

When Dawson confessed that he wanted to get to know her better, it felt as unbelievable as if he had announced that he was Santa Claus. And this wasn't a put-down of herself. Not at all! She believed that she was an attractive person, starting on the inside. But she also knew that she wasn't a Heidi Klum or Sofia Vergara. She had always been a cute "brainy bookworm," a shy girl, but performing from a tender age had made her feel more at home onstage than offstage. Eventually her love for performing and music had even earned her a full-ride scholarship to the prestigious Berklee College of Music in Boston.

During her first year in Boston, she had formed a band with her then roommates named Row House Four, which had played gigs all over the city. The band's success had gone a long way to building her confidence offstage. Many men approached her when their set ended but none of them had been a Dawson John type.

"Thank you again for the hot chocolate," she said.

He smiled at her in a way that made her feel nervous and jittery on the inside. "I'm glad you enjoyed it."

She checked her phone. "My aunt and uncle are expecting me."

Dawson looked reluctant to end their time together, and she felt the same way. But she also knew that she had a big job to do in Bronco and this *spark* they seemed to have between them should be left on the stage, where it could fizzle out on its own.

Before he easily jumped down from where he sat, he put the empty cups in the bag.

"I can help you down," Dawson said to her.

Marisa had the distinct feeling that if she let Dawson John touch her once, even in the most innocent of ways, she was going to keep on letting him touch her in perhaps some *naughty* ways.

"Thanks," she said. "I've got it."

She walked over to the piano, hoisted a heavy backpack on, then grabbed an overstuffed bag filled with sheet music and other tools of her trade.

"Allow me." Dawson reached for the bag.

She handed it to him and found herself smiling at him. She couldn't seem to stop herself from smiling at him!

Together they walked up the stairs, and when they reached the top, Dawson opened the door for her.

"So what's next for you?" he asked.

"After dinner, I'll start sifting through the performers today so I can post them on the theater website tomorrow so I can begin rehearsals."

"So all work, no play?"

"Yes," she said. "But I did enjoy getting to know you."

"Thank you. Me too."

Out in the parking lot, he matched her pace while they walked over to her car.

"Is this a 1982 Ford Falcon?"

"1984." Marisa put her bookbag in the back seat and he followed suit.

"It's completely refurbished," Dawson said, admiring the two-toned silver-and-purple car with its distinctive three windows that together resembled a trapezoid.

"I had a friend in high school who was obsessed with rescuing eighties cars from the junkyard and restoring them. I had some money saved up and he gave me the family discount," she said with a shrug of one shoulder. "Now I am the proud owner of a Ford Falcon.

"Well," she said, opening her door, "I guess I'll see you around?"

"I was actually thinking about stopping by rehearsals."

That surprised her. "I don't typically let the public come to rehearsals. Parents of my young performers, of course, but Charity...*if* she makes the cut, is an adult."

"Can you make one little exception?"

She smiled with a small shake of the head. "I have a feeling that happens quite frequently for you, doesn't it?"

"I'll have to plead the fifth on that one."

"So, I guess I'll see you around?"

"I hope so," he said. "Just do me one favor."

"What's that?"

"If you do allow me to come to rehearsals, please don't kick me out a second time. I do have a reputation to uphold."

She got into the car, tossing him a small smile before closing her door. "I make zero promises."

After his impromptu "date" with Marisa, Dawson headed to the family ranch, the Double J, a sprawling cattle spread located in Bronco Heights, the town's upscale counterpart to Bronco Valley. Whenever he needed to clear his mind and work his way through a problem, he got himself on horseback and went for a long ride. He brushed down a beefy Quarter horse gelding named Scottie.

"How's your day been?" he asked the horse as he picked out his hooves. "Mine's been odd—real odd."

Dawson put the saddle pad on the horse's back, and then swung the saddle over and put it down gently.

Once the bridle was on, Dawson led the horse out of the barn, hooked his left foot into the stirrup, reins in hand, hand resting on the thickly muscled neck of the horse, and then mounted, his right foot finding the stirrup. After a few more tail swishes, Scottie settled down and walked out from Dawson's leg. Dawson didn't have a plan other than *ride until life makes more sense*. Still feeling like that flattened cartoon character, he rode right up until the sun was setting and dusk was upon him. And, after hours of riding, his mind was still bent all out of shape. He wasn't the falling-in-love kind. He certainly didn't go around falling for women who were literally his exact opposite! Marisa Sanchez was an artistic kind of person, and he was definitely *not*! But in spite of it all, Marisa had something special that he must have been unknowingly craving his entire adult life.

It was dusk by the time he returned to the stable. After brushing the sweat from Scottie's back, he handed him over to the stable hand taking care of evening feeding at the barn, and then got in his truck and drove to the main house. What was really eating at him was the undeniable fact that he didn't feel one iota better after his ride. If he was hoping to figure out his strong attraction to Marisa Sanchez, that strategy had failed miserably.

Instead of going through the house where he might have had to talk with his parents, he walked around the long way to the outdoor kitchen that overlooked bucolic, snowy fields that had been harvested for hay stocks as winter was on its way. Dawson found a nice whiskey in the outdoor kitchen, poured himself a glass neat, and then sat down in one of the high quality rocking chairs put there for this exact purpose by his mother, Mimi. It was cold even with his thick, warm coat but he didn't much care. He needed this time alone to think and to figure out how in the hell he had managed to get himself in this mess. He was on his second round of whiskey when the door opened behind him. He looked back over his shoulder, hoping it wasn't his father, Randall, or his mother. They were the last people he wanted to encounter.

"I didn't know you were home." His brother Maddox stepped out onto the lanai.

"Hiding out, big brother," Dawson said. "Buy you a drink?"

"What are you drinking?"

"Whiskey. Neat."

"Can I fill 'er up?"

"Why not?"

Maddox brought the bottle of whiskey over, topped off Dawson's glass before pouring one for himself. His brother took a seat next to him, they clinked glasses, and after taking a deep draw, Maddox made a noise in his throat from the oddly pleasurable burn of whiskey.

"So what's going on?" his brother asked.

Randall and Mimi had four children: Jameson was the eldest, Maddox second in line; Dawson was the third and last brother, while Charity was the only girl and the baby of the family. His parents were wealthy and liked to show it. They also were always trying to climb their way up the social rung to reach the status of the two wealthiest and influential families in Bronco, the Taylors and the Abernathys. And for his parents, part of that competition included their children making acceptable matches when it came time to marry.

"Nothing much," Dawson said pensively.

"Well, that was a load of hogwash right there."

Dawson remained quiet for a bit, and his brother didn't push him. Jameson and Maddox were happily married; Maddox and his wife, Adeline, had given their parents a grandchild, a boy, named Matthew. Did it really matter who Dawson ended up marrying? The fact that he had begun to contemplate the topic of marriage was yet another layer of *what the hell is going on*?

"I'm here if you want to talk about it, Dawson."

"Honestly?" he said after draining his glass and putting it down on a side table. "I don't even know where to begin."

"That doesn't sound good."

"No," Dawson agreed. "It doesn't."

Maddox looked at him with an intense gaze. "Now you've got me worried."

Dawson didn't respond.

"What's this about, D? Seriously. Now I've got to know so I can help you if I can. Please tell me you haven't gotten someone pregnant...?"

That question made him chuckle—that would be worse than falling in love with a woman who didn't meet the Randall and Mimi standards for their children, all in the pursuit of reaching that top rung on the food chain.

"No." He smiled at the thought. "It's not that."

"Well, thank heaven above for that." Maddox poured himself another whiskey. "But it does have something to do with a woman?"

Dawson gave a small nod and put his empty glass off to the side.

"Not a woman who would pass our parents' *Marry debutantes from other cattle families*?"

"That's about the size of it."

They shared a comfortable silence. His brothers weren't just siblings, they were his best friends. And Dawson knew he could trust Maddox explicitly.

"Let me run something by you."

"Shoot," Maddox said.

"From my way of seeing it, Charity is the princess," he said. "Jameson is the heir. You're the spare."

"Mom and Dad would love you using all of these royal family terms." Maddox laughed. "What does that make you?"

"It makes me *I don't care.*"

Maddox laughed out loud before he said, "Well, you may not care, little brother. But I guarantee this—Randall and Mimi sure as hell *will* care."

"Yeah. I know," Dawson conceded. "But we love who we love and if they don't fit neatly into that 'daughters of cattle barons only' box, that's when changes need to be made."

His brother looked at him with both concern and shock, "Love?"

"Maybe," Dawson said with an image of Marisa's sweet face and sparkling eyes in the forefront of his mind. "Just maybe."

Maddox leaned toward him, looking at him straight on, "If there's someone you want, Dawson. Someone that you know, in the deepest part of your soul, that you love, just put on your armor and prepare yourself for battle. That's the best advice I can give you."

Chapter Three

Dawson had awakened the next morning with a slight hangover and to an irate text from Natasha, telling him to lose her number after he stood her up on the same day he had asked her out. He felt bad about it—he really did—and he apologized, but he was pretty sure that she had blocked him. But in his defense, Marisa Sanchez had kicked his legs right out from underneath him. How could he be expected to go out on a date after those impactful encounters with Marisa? After trying to make things right with Natasha, Dawson jumped in the shower. He had hoped that he would wake up right back to his old familiar, carefree, pre-Marisa life. That didn't happen. Now, all he could think to do was get that pass to attend rehearsals once they got started.

"You look tired, Dawson," his mother commented when he joined his parents at the table for breakfast. "And I think you need a haircut."

"I'll look into it," he said while he filled his plate with stick-to-your-ribs breakfast fare that his mother had prepared for them.

Halfway through his second helping, Charity burst into the room and raised her hands above her head and said in a very happy voice, "I did it! I'm in the Mistletoe Pageant!"

Dawson was happy to have his mother's attention switch from him to his golden-haired baby sister.

"That's real nice." Randall turned down the corner of the newspaper to look at his daughter. "Congratulations."

Mimi smiled at her daughter while carefully buttering a piece of toast for her husband. "That's wonderful, sweetheart, but I'd go easy on breakfast if I were you. You know what they say. A moment on the lips…"

Some of Charity's initial excitement waned and Dawson felt for her. Their parents were well-meaning, but they sometimes managed to dampen any good news with cautionary tales. Dawson got up, hugged Charity and congratulated her.

"What role will you have?" Mimi asked as she handed her husband the toast.

Charity sat down and gave herself big helpings of eggs, sausage patties, cheese grits and a biscuit. Dawson smiled as he poured his sister a full-to-the-rim glass of orange juice and then passed her the honey.

"I have one solo, one group song, and I'll be in the whole choir performances. *And* I am in two dance numbers. One number will include Bollywood moves!"

Randall lowered the paper again, stared at her over the rim of his reading glasses and asked, "Now what are you going to be doing?"

"I watched some Bollywood movies and they are so bright and energetic. But how would that work with our traditional Christmas songs?" Mimi's lips were pursed disapprovingly. "I don't think I like the sound of that at all."

"Well, some of the Christmas songs won't have traditional music arrangements. Instead their arrangements will be influenced by jazz, rock, Motown, and even hip-hop."

"No. That's a terrible idea!" their mom exclaimed.

"Times change, Mom. And we have to change with them," Charity said.

"That's a matter of opinion, little one," Randall said, returning to his paper.

"I for one am thrilled to see the pageant evolve," his sister said. "I'm proud to be a part of it. How do you feel about it, Dawson?"

"Me?" he asked, drinking down a third glass of orange juice. "I feel great about it. Can't wait to attend."

"Thank you, Dawson." She smiled at him.

"You are most welcome, Charity." He winked at her. They were overacting for sure, but this game was one that all of the John kids played to good-naturedly tweak their parents a bit.

The more she talked about her roles in the pageant, the more concerned her mother's face became. Mimi seemed unimpressed with direction of the once "set in stone" traditional Mistletoe Pageant.

Mimi folded her napkin and put it on her plate. "I'm very happy that you will play a large role in the pageant because you sing like an angel and you look like an angel."

"Thank you, Mom."

She held up a finger to stop her daughter. "But I am very concerned about what I'm hearing. Why in the world would the committee hire someone to run the pageant who isn't even from Bronco? And I don't think her idea is the right direction for our Mistletoe Pageant. We need the classics that are part of our tradition. That's what Bronco wants. That's what Bronco expects."

"I'm not positive, but I think there will be classic Christmas carols," Charity explained.

Her mom continued with a heavy sigh. "I want you to be happy, Charity, you know I do. I will be there in the front row cheering you on. But I'm afraid this new idea is doomed to fail. There is no way the Abernathys or the Taylors will stand for this."

Dawson left the breakfast table feeling unsettled about his parents' reaction to the direction Marisa was taking the Mistletoe Pageant. He supposed it made sense that he felt protective of the Tenacity native because she had stolen his heart with just one look. What he saw was a train wreck unfolding in slow motion before his very eyes, and he was at a loss as to how to stop the crash from happening. Marisa was in real danger of having a revolt on her hands. Yes, there was a solid faction of young Broncoites who were more flexible and willing to buck tradition, but others, especially the old guard, could be as inflexible and unyielding as stainless steel. When news got out that Marisa was turning the whole Mistletoe production on its head, Dawson could absolutely see a boycott of the entire show by the old guard. He didn't want to see this happen for a multitude of reasons: he loved his town and the holiday season and he didn't want to see anything ruin that tradition for Bronco. He also didn't want his sister to get caught in the cross fire. But perhaps more importantly, and certainly more selfishly, Dawson did not want Marisa to become persona non grata in Bronco before he had even managed to ask her out for their first date!

"I've got to find a way to get through to her," Dawson told himself as he got behind the wheel of his GMC Denali Ultimate. "Somehow, someway, I've got to open Marisa's eyes to the reality of Bronco. For her sake and for mine."

Marisa had awakened the morning after the auditions feeling exhausted but determined. She was grateful that her uncle Aaron and aunt Denise had allowed her to crash at their house in Bronco Valley. From the minute she walked in their door, the smell of good food cooking in the kitchen made her feel right at home. She knew that she had a safe harbor to dock her boat during her short stay in Bronco. She posted the list of performers who would have roles in the production. She also included a list for those who did not earn roles to help with building the sets. Then, she spent the day with her extended Bronco family to recharge for the first day of rehearsals.

The next day, she was greeted warmly by Agnes.

"Welcome back!" Agnes beamed at her. "How are you feeling?"

Marisa shrugged out of her jacket nd then took off her gloves and winter hat. "Thank you, Agnes. I feel pretty good. I wish I'd managed to get more sleep, but my mind was whirling with song arrangements and dance sequences! On the down side, I have some real concerns about the timeline."

"Let's go have a nice cup of coffee and let's see if we can muddle our way through some of your concerns."

Marisa followed Agnes to the kitchenette backstage, once again feeling grateful that Agnes had taken such an interest in the pageant.

"I'm sorry I don't have hot chocolate." Agnes put a cup of freshly made coffee down in front of Marisa before joining her at the table. "I forgot to stop by the store today."

Marisa blew on her coffee. "Please don't go out of your way just for that. A hot cup of coffee is wonderful. Thank you."

"So," Agnes said, "let me have it. We can troubleshoot together."

Marisa breathed in deeply and then let out a long sigh. "I'm just out of my depth here, Agnes. If I had more time,

I wouldn't have any trouble pulling this off. My mom will be coming in from Tenacity tomorrow to measure the performers for their costumes. She always makes the costumes for my shows."

"Good news."

"Yes," Marisa agreed. "The local band has already been practicing the updated versions of some Christmas classics. They've sent me videos, and that's actually going better than expected. They are so talented."

Agnes listened, giving her a nod every now and again to let her know that she was listening.

"But," she continued, "in three weeks, the singers need to be hitting all of their marks with unfamiliar arrangements, and I have to manage to teach people who don't dance how to dance in ways completely new to them. As for the sets, I have some of the sets that I use in my Tenacity holiday show stored in my aunt and uncle's garage, and so many people signed up to help with that. It's just a lot. When I organize and direct the holiday show in Tenacity, I've known almost everyone for years and we work together like clockwork.

"But I don't have that here. I know from experience that it can be super challenging to work with people I haven't worked with before. Rapport usually takes time that is not an abundant resource right now." Marisa sat back in her chair and asked, more to herself than to Agnes, "Did I bite off more than I can chew with this job? Does Bronco always have such a tight timeline?"

"Okay, last question answered first. Yes, we always have a tight timeline, but because we're always putting on the same ol' pageant with the same ol' singers and dancers, we don't need a whole lot of time."

"And now I'm shaking things up."

"In more ways than one." Agnes gave a nod. "And to your first question, no you haven't bit off more than you can chew. Rapport can be built quickly if you're kind. And from what I saw during rehearsals, you are kind and supportive and caring, and I know each and every one of those performers, young to old, and they will work hard for you—just as hard as I know you will work for them."

"Well, thank you, Agnes. You give good pep talks."

"I call it as I see it."

Marisa stood up, pushed in her chair, rinsed out her cup and set it aside. And then something other than rehearsals came to mind.

"By the way…"

Agnes was busily sweeping the floor. "Yes?"

"Guess who stopped by the other day bearing the gift of hot chocolate and marshmallows?"

A very sheepish expression appeared on Agnes's face. She stopped sweeping, leaned on the broom handle and said, "I have no idea."

That made Marisa laugh, and it felt good to laugh. Calmed her nerves a bit.

"But," Agnes said, "did it work?"

"Did I accept the apology?"

"Did you?"

Marisa laughed. "Of course it did! When Adonis in a Stetson shows up with hot chocolate and marshmallows, you forgive!"

"He is such a handsome man," Agnes said with parental-like pride. "I had him for kindergarten to fifth grade for music."

Marisa couldn't stop herself from asking, "What was he like as a boy?"

"Darling, cute as a button, mischievous…" the older

woman said, then turned back to her work. "Now go have yourself a great rehearsal, Marisa! And don't forget to have a good time. Otherwise, what's this all for?"

Marisa did feel better after her talk with Agnes, and she walked out onto the stage to greet the performers already gathered in the theater seats. Her gaze naturally went up to where she had first laid eyes on Dawson, but he wasn't there. And she felt disappointed. Maybe he hadn't enjoyed their meet-cute as much as she had. Dawson John and all he had to offer had played tug-of-war in her mind, fighting for her attention while she was in the casting process and during her restless sleep. Her brain had found a balance, sharing the time pretty equally split between Dawson and plans for the Mistletoe Pageant.

Her disappointment was fleeting as her excited jitters for the first day of rehearsals propelled her to the edge of the stage. With a genuine smile on her face, she opened her arms wide as a welcoming gesture and called out to audience, "Good afternoon, Mistletoe Pageant performers!"

She began to hand out packets of songs and began to review them with the singers. The groups broke off and began to read over their songs and parts. They got Now that rehearsals were underway, Marisa made the rounds and worked with individuals or groups to rehearse the show. Marisa could see right away that she had passionate, hard workers in the boat with her and they were all prepared to row the boat with her.

"Hi!" Charity John took a straight line to her and gave her a huge hug. "Thank you for believing in me. I won't let you down."

"I do believe in you, Charity. Now it's time for you to believe in yourself."

When Charity arrived alone without her brother Marisa had to push aside her renewed disappointment.

"The show must go on," she said quietly to herself. And, truthfully, he wasn't her type and she was pretty certain that she wasn't his, and this attraction he felt for her could be an anomaly not a total change of heart. Her disappointment came from a place in her heart that wasn't the least bit rational. That's why she needed to acknowledge it— and *ignore* it.

Charity took the stage, her hands gripping the pages of her solo parts as she stood on her mark.

Marisa sat down at the piano and began to play Charity's solo in a modernized rendition of "Let it Snow." Charity's first, second and third attempt were shaky and pitchy. And, Marisa could see that Charity was becoming frustrated to the point of wanting to walk off the stage. So, Marisa left the piano and walked over to the stage and gave her some tips on posture and breath control. Charity was about to try to put the tips into practice when her shoulders slumped even lower as she said, "Great. Just what I needed."

Marisa turned and saw Dawson standing just inside the door; he raised his eyebrows at her and she nodded "yes" to his question. She had to turn away from him so she didn't start staring and even thought Charity was noticeably frustrated by her brother's appearance, *her* heart was beating as fast as a humming bird's wings. That man had an effect on her that was beyond her control to stop.

"Will you please excuse me?" Charity asked.

Marisa nodded and returned to her piano bench. Some-how, sitting at the piano gave her something to focus on other than Dawson while she insisted that her brain *stop* paying so much mind to that cowboy!

"What are you doing here?" his sister asked him in an annoyed tone.

Dawson pulled up straight and gave her a grin. "I thought you'd like me to be here on your first rehearsal day."

His baby sister frowned at him. "Well, I don't. But since you're already here, make sure you turn off your phone!"

"Already did it."

"And don't clap or cheer for me." She pointed at him. "Not one word! Not one peep out of you or I will have Agnes remove you from this theater and ban you for life!"

"What about the Mistletoe Pageant?"

"Banned for life!" Charity raised her voice, something that was out of character for her.

"I'll be on my best behavior," he said sincerely. "I promise."

Charity gave him a sour look before she turned on her heel and quickly returned to the stage. She wasn't the only one who ignored him. After their first eye contact, Marisa did not look at him even when he tried to will Marisa to look over at him, to throw him a bone, but she didn't and it irked him! He hadn't experienced that before and he certainly didn't like how it felt In just a short amount of time, Dawson realized that Marisa was fiercely independent, talented, kindhearted, and a take-charge type of woman. How did one approach a woman like her?

"Carefully," he whispered under his breath. "Very carefully."

After watching the rehearsal, Dawson was amazed not only at what Marisa was doing with the show, but with his sister. She really shined onstage, and he was so proud of her. "You were amazing, peanut." Dawson used his child-hood nickname for his sister. "I've never heard you sound like that before."

"Thank you," Charity said, slipping on her jacket, which she had laid across a nearby chair. "Marisa is a musical genius. The way she explains things! The way she mod-els what she wants me to do, it's beyond. She's on a whole different level."

"You get some of that credit too, you know."

"I know." She nodded. "But Mom has had me in lessons as soon as I began to talk it seems like. In over ten years of lessons, not one of my coaches got me to where Marisa just did in fifteen minutes."

Charity zipped up her jacket, threw a backpack over one shoulder and then looked at him. "Are you coming with?"

Dawson had been wondering exactly how to get by with his "romance Marisa" plan without Charity noticing, and then he realized he couldn't. She was too smart and too observant.

"No," he said. "I think I'm going to stick around."

She narrowed her eyes. "Why?"

His eyes moved past his sister to watch Marisa work-ing on a song at the piano. Charity must have followed his gaze because she let out a harsh whisper. "No. *No!* You have women all over the state of Montana ready to worship at the feet of the incredibly handsome, athletic and wealthy Dawson John! Leave Marisa alone!"

"I just want to get to know her, Charity. Nothing more to it than that."

Charity balled up her hands into fists, squeezed them tightly and then said, "If you screw this up for me, Daw-son, I promise you I will never forgive you. You have no idea how much this means to me."

"I think I might," he said gently. "I'm not going to do anything to hurt you."

"But you might do something to hurt Marisa."

Dawson wanted to reassure his baby sister that he had no intention to hurt Marisa in the pursuit of love. How could he? In all of his thirty years, he now knew that he hadn't ever been in love. Not really and not like this. Hell, for all he knew, *he* could be the one who'd be left with a broken heart.

Charity studied him with worried eyes. "I can't change your mind."

"No," he said. "Not on this one."

Charity hooked arm through the other strap on her backpack so it was held evenly between both arms. "At least promise me that you will tread lightly, Dawson. She's... special."

"I promise," he said sincerely. "I promise you that I will."

Chapter Four

"Hi, Dawson." Marisa stopped at the last row and greeted him with a sincere, kind smile that reached her lovely dark brown eyes. They were the last ones left and he preferred it that way. An audience could complicate this budding friendship in ways that he imagined could have Marisa running as far away from him as humanly possible.

He had a reputation as a playboy and people gossiped about him—a lot. He hated to think what they might say if they saw him chatting up the new girl in town. He didn't pay attention to the chatter, but Marisa *might*, and he was willing to bet she wouldn't like it.

"Hi, Marisa." He stood up and took her bag off her shoulder and put it onto his. "Do you have time for coffee? Tea?"

"Or me?" she asked teasingly.

"Whoa! Slow down, Ms. Sanchez. I'm a slow burn, not a flash in the pan," he said, grabbing his Stetson from a coatrack and putting it back on his head.

That made her laugh and he loved the sound of it.

"I'm always in the mood for hot chocolate," she told him.

"I know a place with excellent hot chocolate and abundant marshmallows."

"Lead the way, kind sir."

Together they walked to the parking lot and then to her Falcon.

"Are we walking or driving?" she asked.

"Driving. I wouldn't mind a ride in your car. It's cool."

Marisa tossed her thick curls over her shoulder sassily and titled her head flirtatiously. "Of course it is. Didn't you get the memo, Dawson? *I'm* super cool."

Marisa cranked the engine and asked, "Where to?"

"Take a left and then drive for a piece."

"As the crow flies?" she bantered, enjoying his company as if she had known him for a long time.

"Spoken like a Montana girl."

"Well—" she turned onto the road "—I'm from here. Just down the road, you know."

Dawson turned toward her, admiring the smooth ride of the vehicle. "I've heard that, yeah."

"Born and raised in Tenacity, an hour or so away from Bronco. Maybe it isn't everyone's cup of tea, but it's my own little slice of heaven on Earth."

"It's good to love where you come from."

"Yes, it is."

After a short silence, Marisa said, "Your shoulders take up too much room in my Falcon! It never felt small before."

He winked at her. "I've never had any complaints. I've been told my shoulders are one of my best features."

"What are your worst features?"

Dawson rubbed his chin, pretending to be in serious thought. "Now that you ask, I'd be hard-pressed to find one."

"May I suggest that enormous ego as a possible flaw?" she asked. "I bet that's what's taking up all the space in here! Roll down the window and let me have some air!"

Their conversation turned to small talk and then Dawson pointed to a little roadside greasy spoon and a gas station on the outskirts of town that didn't appear to get a lot of customers.

Marisa pulled in to a spot and turned off the engine. She looked at the restaurant with curiosity. "Eat, Gas-n-Go? This is the place?"

"This *is* the place."

She took the key out of the ignition. "Okay."

Dawson took his hat off the dashboard, stepped out of the car, put his hat back on and said, "Hold up! Let me be a gentleman and open up your door."

"Okay," she said, "if you want to."

"Lately, I do," he said. He walked quickly to her side of the Falcon, held out his hand for her to take and helped her out.

"Thank you."

"You're welcome."

They walked in together and the decor was sixties chic with real splatters of grease and some handprints of children on the newsprint wallpaper peeling off the wall.

They were greeted by an older gentleman with an unlit, half-smoked cigarette stuck to his lip.

"Take your pick." The man nodded toward the three tables with faded blue tops and orange scoop benches. "Menu's on the table."

She sat down and looked around with a pleased smile. "I love this kind of place."

"Me too." Dawson pulled on a menu that was stuck to another one. He peeled them apart and handed Marisa hers.

"Hungry?" he asked.

"I am, but my aunt and uncle expect me to eat a healthy

meal with them," she explained but scanned the menu for another time.

"Ready?" the man asked.

Dawson put the menus back in their holder and held up two fingers. "Two hot chocolates, heavy on the marshmallows."

In no time at all, the man delivered their drinks, and her large mug was overflowing with marshmallows that were already melting into the hot chocolate.

Dawson held up his mug. "What should we toast to?"

"A successful pageant!"

They touched mugs. "Here's to the most amazing Mistletoe Pageant Bronco has ever seen."

Marisa took that first wonderful sip of the chocolatey beverage and closed her eyes to fully enjoy the feeling of the warmth spreading from her mouth to her belly. When she opened her eyes, Dawson was studying her.

"I've never seen anyone enjoy hot chocolate like you do."

"Well," she said, "maybe you've never met anyone like me before."

"Now that's the darn truth." He smiled at her in a way that made her blush and feel a tad insecure.

She put her hands on her mug to warm them. "Let me ask you something."

"Shoot."

"I may not know Bronco very well, but I'm sure there are a few places to get hot chocolate without the long drive. Why'd you pick this place?"

Without any hesitation, he said, "It's away from prying eyes. I have a way of finding myself the topic of the gossip column in the local newspaper a time or ten. It's not a lot of fun."

She took another wonderful sip of the drink. "Oh. That

makes sense. And thank you, actually. I'm not sure I want to draw attention to myself other than for my role as the director of the pageant."

"You're welcome, then. I'm glad I got it right."

"You did." She smiled at him. "One of my videos from Tenacity's last Christmas choir went viral on TikTok…"

"Charity mentioned that…"

"I didn't expect it, and it still feels weird when someone outside of my circle recognizes me. I have so many new followers and that I don't mind, but I did become a bit of a celebrity in Tenacity."

She showed Dawson the video that had started the whole "local celebrity" deal. "Actually, this video actually got me this job."

"How so?"

"The committee for the pageant heard about my arrangements of holiday classics, and next thing you know, here I am!"

"Well," he said, "thank you, TikTok."

Marisa didn't quite know how to respond to Dawson's out in the open interest in her. She liked it and she liked him. She could even concede that they made sense in a greasy spoon on the outskirts of town, but in town *out there* with all of their friends and family involved? That couldn't make sense.

"You have a marshmallow mustache," he told her.

"So do you."

He opened his phone, turned the camera around to look at himself and he said, "Gosh darn. You're right. Come on over here and let's get a picture."

Laughing, she came over to his side and sat down next to him. He put his arm around her and then held out the phone and took a picture of them to immortalize their twin marshmallow mustaches.

"It's a good picture," she said.

"Agreed. We look good together," Dawson said, pulling up his Instagram and pushing buttons, leading her to believe that he was really going to post that picture while she watched in absolute horror.

"Wait!" she said in a loud voice. "You aren't going to post that, are you?"

"Well, I was."

She shook her head. "No."

He looked confused. "Why not?"

Marisa returned to her side of the table, leaned her body forward and said, "You can't post that!"

He waited for her to explain.

"Dawson! I've already told you that TikTok changed my life in ways both good and bad. Once that content is out there, it's out there for *life*."

When he still didn't look convinced, she told him to close Instagram, and after he did, she sat back relieved and then asked, "Tell me the truth. Am I someone you would typically go for?"

He didn't respond.

"Okay. Bad question. How's this. I don't want to hurt your feelings, but *you* would be a seismic shift in my social media," she said, "and even though I haven't poked around in your social media…"

"Hurt."

"But I very much doubt that I would see too many Marisas."

"There's only one Marisa."

"Dawson! I'm serious."

"So was I…" he said. "And who cares anyway?"

"For one, I do!" she said. "I have friends who have dated

for six months before they post. It's almost as serious as an engagement announcement." Dawson seemed deflated and that made her feel sad. "That doesn't mean we can't still be friends."

After a silence, Dawson said, "If we are seen together in Bronco, we could end up in the paper."

"Well, I don't want to have all of the mothers of eligible daughters hating me and boycotting the show. But if we are just having innocent fun and we end up in the paper, at least it will stay *local*, not like social media."

After another silence, he said, "Okay. We'll do it your way. You have a point, anyway. The folks who write about me in the paper would probably take note if I posted marshmallow mustache pics with a beautiful stranger in town."

"We can't build a bubble around us. But we can pick and choose some ways that we put ourselves out there."

"Agreed."

Marisa checked her own phone and saw that she had forgotten to turn her phone from silent to vibrate and had missed both a call and a text from her aunt.

"I've got to get back," she said.

Dawson took out his wallet and put money on the table. "Okay, let's get you back."

On the way to town, Dawson felt odd inside, like his skin didn't fit him any longer. He was an adrenaline junkie, always had been and most likely always would be. But sitting in that diner with Marisa felt like a new untapped adrenaline. The shiny silkiness of her hair made him want to comb his fingers through it and feel it on his skin. Her lips were full and those dark eyes, so insightful and kind, cut straight through to his soul. She was a curvaceous woman he thought her curves were beautiful and sexy and enticing; and that made him realize that what he was feeling for Marisa went way beyond the physical. This was uncharted territory for him and that tipped him off balance.

With so many obvious differences between them, and no doubt a dump truck load of differences yet to be uncovered, Dawson just didn't know how to capture the heart of a woman like Marisa Sanchez. But he wanted to learn.

"You're awfully quiet," Marisa said as she drove them back into town. "Everything okay?"

"Sure," he said, not wanting to overwhelm her with the very serious thoughts he was having about her. He did not want to scare Marisa away by coming on to strong. He needed to slow down, give her time to get to know him.

"So," she said, "what do you think about the show so far? I mean obviously it's the first day and that's always hectic and jumbled."

That question hung in the air between them and when she glanced over at him, awaiting his response, he did his best to be diplomatic. "I think the first rehearsal went well."

She nodded and waited, no doubt catching the subtle hesitation before landing on "well."

"And what you did with Charity—honestly, it was like you gave her a fifteen minute master class. I've never heard her sound like that before."

She continued to nod and wait, giving him all the space he needed to give her an appraisal.

"But…"

She raised her eyebrows. "But…?"

"I think," he said slowly, wishing he could go back in time and cut this encounter short before she could pin him down on his opinion. Unfortunately, he was trapped in her car and he had no where to go. All roads led to bad news. "And, this is only because you are new to Bronco and Bronco hasn't had time to adjust—"

"Adjust?"

Damn it! Wrong word. Wrong word!

He took in a big breath and blew it out slowly; it was the sigh of a defeated man. "There might be some people in town—you know, people who prefer their holidays 'classic'—" Dawson made finger quotes around the word "—and are resistant to change. I just wonder how they gonna feel about some of the changes you're making to the pageant."

He could see the furrow in her brow and new the wheels were spinning out of control in her head. "What does this Bronco old guard have to do with my rehearsal?"

At the look on Marisa's face, Dawson felt like those weird trapezoid Falcon windows were closing in on him.

Marisa's eyebrows furrowed. "But that's why I was hired! Someone here saw my videos from last year's Tenacity holiday show and the committee hired me to *start* new traditions. Why would the town council hire me if they *didn't* want a refresh?!"

Marisa's voice had raised and she was gripping the steering wheel tightly. He *knew* talking about the pageant was going to ruin what had been a nice time together.

Not another word was spoken between them until they arrived at the theater parking lot and she parked and turned off the engine. Staring out of the windshield, Marisa was frowning deeply, her eyes confused and concerned, and he felt as if the progress he had just made with the pretty director had just been swept away.

"No." She shook her head. "That can't be."

He didn't know the right words to say so he remained quiet.

She looked into his face and studied him carefully. "Is

your family a part of this group of people that don't like change?"

"Yeah. They are." What else could he say? He had to tell her the truth even if it meant she backed away from him. If Marisa ever caught him lying, he felt instinctively that Marisa would shut him down and never let him back in.

"Is that how you feel?" she asked.

"No. But, I do think that too much change over a very short time will not go over well in Bronco. The Mistletoe Pageant is hallowed ground."

"Then why hire me? I just don't get it."

"Look," he said, "I could be wrong."

"That's true." She nodded with a hopeful expression. "You could be."

"Maybe we could figure out exactly how Bronco feels."

"How?"

"We make a wager."

"What are the terms?"

"How about you have a pop-up concert in the park across from the city hall. This time of year, there are a lot of people passing through the park, watching the city begin the routine of putting up Christmas decorations downtown."

"I could set up my portable keyboard."

"You could alternate between modern takes on Christmas songs and then classic takes."

"Maybe the same song back-to-back?"

"Sure," he said, "why not?"

"I wonder if Charity would be willing to be my accompaniment?"

"She'd do it. I'm sure she would. She thinks that you can walk on water."

"I just love her so much already," Marisa said sincerely while she held out her hand to him.

After some moments of thought, Marisa said, "It's not the worst idea I've ever heard."

"Gee, thanks?" He said half in jest. Marisa did not give him any leeway he had grown accustomed to from the opposite sex.

"You're welcome," Marisa said and then asked, "What would I win? I do feel confident that I *will* win."

"Besides the invaluable knowledge gained from the focus group? The loser takes the other one out to dinner."

"Full disclosure. I have a bologna budget."

"I know a great burger place."

"Or a greasy spoon on the outskirts of town where you can eat *and* get your tires rotated?"

That made him smile; he found himself smiling quite a bit with the lovely Miss Sanchez.

"If you win, you choose."

Marisa gave a shrug. "I'm pretty sure I'll win."

He loved the fact that he had turned the conversation around and now Marisa, a woman who liked to win, was fully invested in this wager and not stuck on whether she could win over some stuffy ranchers.

"All right, Dawson John. I'm in. Tomorrow in the park. Afternoon after rehearsals, so it won't be impossibly cold. Get ready to lose."

"I'll look forward to it." He winked at her and smiled to let her know that he was being ironic. He believed, without a shadow of doubt, that he would win. Either way, win or lose, he was the winner—he had managed to find a way to share a meal with the object of his sudden-onset affection.

The next afternoon, after a rigorous day of rehearsals, Marisa rode with Charity to Bronco Park. She had been disappointed when Dawson hadn't come to watch the rehearsals and was looking forward to seeing him in the park. He was beyond handsome, a real, living Greek god in human form, and she had judged him unfairly. She had assumed that he would be completely off-putting and shallow. If he had those sides of his personality from a lifetime of getting what he wanted based on his looks alone, he didn't show them to her.

"I love this park!" Marisa exclaimed. "It seems so odd to me that I visited my aunt and uncle several times when I was growing up, but I don't remember them ever bringing me here."

Charity parked her truck and shut off the engine. "This park and all of downtown is transformed into a Christmas wonderland. This time of year we have so many musicians and carolers performing in this park. When I was growing up, and during my beauty pageant days, I sang here sometimes."

"Well, that's good news. You can show me the ropes."

"Of course I will," Charity said sweetly. "Oh, here comes Dawson now."

And there it was, that same nervous stomach, that same shallow breathing and tingling sensations in her lips, fingers and toes. The mental fluctuation were annoying—one minute she was ready to enjoy a fun, casual, short and sweet holiday romance with Dawson and the next she wanted to push him away so she wouldn't get too attached. The part that wanted to push him away was the part of her that knew Dawson John, as much as she enjoyed his easy company, was not the type of man she would seriously pursue as a possible love match.

They came from backgrounds so different that they may as well have been raised on different planets. Perhaps they could have some fun, make a few memories, and perhaps, let this undeniable chemistry between them play out as a holiday tryst. But could she imagine a long-term romance with him? *No.* She was convinced that she would not fit fully into his world and she was pretty certain her way of life, one of hard work and community service, would grow tiresome for a man like Dawson in less than a month's time.

"Hey there, ladies." Dawson smiled at them.

Charity hugged her brother quickly.

"Seems like a perfect day to win a wager!" Dawson rubbed his hands together.

"Well, thank you, Dawson," Marisa gave him a cheeky smile. "Are you already accepting your defeat?"

"Not a chance!" he countered. "What can I help you with?"

Dawson carried her portable keyboard while she carried her stool and sheet music, and Charity carried a case full of tambourines and bells.

Dawson and Charity helped her get set up and then she put an old coffee can on the top of her keyboard. She donned a Santa hat that matched her Santa scarf and her Christmas tree sweater that had actual blinking lights.

Dawson had been watching her again, and one side of his lovely lips were turned up in a crooked smile that only added to his already ridiculous handsomeness.

"Are we ready?" Marisa sat down on her stool.

"Ready," Charity said, holding two silver bells in her gloved hands.

"What's my role?" Dawson asked.

"You need to find us some people," Marisa said, as she handed him a small container of red chips and blue chips.

"Poker chips." He smiled. "Where'd you pick up these?"

"Turns out Agnes loves a poker night." She laughed. "So,

reindeer red will be for classic arrangements and sleigh bell blue will be for a modern take on holiday classics."

"You don't play around." Dawson whistled, clearly impressed by her plan to tally the town's preference.

"Not when it comes to work," she said. "The results of this focus group will inform my decisions for the show. I really don't think that the good people of Bronco will side with you. But we shall see!"

"I do want to apologize right up front for the loss you are about to experience." Dawson flashed a teasing smile.

"Cocky. I hope you're not a sore loser." She teased back and then said, "People choose the colored chip that corresponds to their preference and then drop it into this coffee can right here. Is that clear?"

"I think I've got it," Dawson said, still in a teasing tone. "May the best man win."

Charity rolled her eyes at her brother, "You're the only man here, Dawson."

"I know. I'm the best man here right now, so I guess I'll be taking home a win. Get it?"

Marisa said to Charity, "Let's see how this man will take defeat when the two best women win."

"He'll probably cry," his sister said.

"You know what? I thought that about him when I first saw him." Marisa nodded. "A very big crier."

Dawson couldn't seem to take his eyes off Marisa; she looked adorable in her Santa hat, scarf and ugly Christmas sweater. When she played the keyboard, she emitted a joyousness that seem to come from her very soul. She loved making music and he loved watching her perform. Yes, he had known she was an incredible musician, but he hadn't yet heard her sing more than a few notes as an example for the singers auditioning for her. The way her voice sounded with its crystal clear pitch and roundness of the notes, he found himself mesmerized by her.

"Dawson!" Charity sent him a disapproving look. "You're supposed to be bringing us voters! Quit ogling Marisa!"

Dawson rarely felt embarrassed, but the fact that he was caught gazing at Marisa and listening to her sing a jazzed-up version of "White Christmas," by his baby sister no less, he got a very large taste of embarrassment and he didn't like the way it made him feel at all.

"Well," he said sheepishly, "you shouldn't be singing so pretty if you wanted me to be able to work."

Marisa smiled at him in a way that put him at ease like no one in his life had ever done before. He had grown up with type A personality parents who pushed all of their four kids to constantly strive for an impossible level of perfection. Randall and Mimi love their children but the high expectations they had for their children felt too heavy to carry. Perhaps that was what he had always rebelled against.

The kindness and acceptance that Dawson felt with just one simple look from Marisa had not been something he was accustomed to. His parents had mainly showed their love for their children with the best material objects that money could buy. And in that moment, he wondered if Marisa's more humble upbringing, just based on what he knew of her aunt and uncle, was the better option for raising children.

"Dawson!" Charity yelled at him with her eyes wide and questioning with a hint of disapproval mixed in.

"Get ready to buy my dinner!" Marisa called after him. "And Charity's dinner too!"

Chapter Five

It was overcast and cold in the park; it looked like a snow sky to her. And, even though she was wearing gloves with the tips of the fingers exposed, her hands were beginning to ache.

"How are you doing?" Charity asked.

"My fingers are cramping up," she admitted.

"Should we take a break? Or call it a day?"

Charity John was such a sweet, dear young woman and, in her mind, that light reflected on Dawson. They were raised in the same family, so Dawson couldn't be completely different. Could he?

"And why do you even care?" she asked out loud.

"Would you repeat that?" Charity asked.

"I was just wondering if your brother would tip the scales in his favor."

"No," Charity said. "He's competitive and doesn't like to lose…"

"Me either."

"But he's not a liar and he's not a cheater."

"Well, that's good know."

Charity stopped playing the bells and walked over to her. She took one look at her exposed fingers, which had begun to turn white.

"No. This has to stop." Charity took off her own gloves to feel Marisa's hands. "Your fingers feel like ice cubes. We need to get them warmed up. Let's call it quits before you get frostbite!"

"No." Marisa dug in her heels. "This is important to me, Charity. I need to know what Bronco wants—classic, modern, a mixture of both?"

"Well, then, at least take a break," Charity suggested.

"Okay," Marisa agreed. "I can do that. But I don't want to leave my instruments."

"I'll stay here," Charity said before she yelled for her brother to come over.

Dawson turned, looked over at them before he quickly left the small group of people with whom he was talking and walked with long strides over to his sister and Marisa.

"What's wrong?"

"Nothing really." Marisa downplayed the situation.

Charity disagreed. "It's something. Her fingers are ice cold but she won't call it quits."

"Stubborn," Dawson said, concern present on his face. "How about we scrounge up some hot chocolate for you?"

Marisa gave in; she hated it, but she knew it was the best thing for her to do in that moment. She wasn't giving up, she was just taking a break from the focus group.

Dawson put down the chips and offered her his arm; he was always a gentleman with her and while she appreciated it and found it charming, she didn't accept it. She looked up into his gorgeous face just in time to see a flash of rejection in his striking eyes.

"Thank you, Dawson," she said to soften the blow. "I think we should stick to our agreement from yesterday. Keep it casual while the good people of Bronco get to know me better."

Dawson's lips turned down. "Maybe I overplayed my hand. I don't want you to get the wrong idea. Bronco is a friendly town. Always has been. Just some are more tied to our traditions than others."

She reached over and touched his arm. "No. I'm grateful that you told me. In all seriousness, I don't like to be wrong, but I may very well be wrong. I was hired because of my popular TikTok videos, but that doesn't mean that my take on the classics and will work here. What if ticket sales are down because of my modern approach? I would be truly horrified and incredibly sad if I did anything to ruin the show that is the kickoff for the whole holiday season! Especially this year because Agnes told me that part of the proceeds of ticket sales this year is going to fund a summer theatre camp!"

Dawson gave a slight nod that signaled to her that he had heard her. He was pensive for the short walk to a small, locally owned coffee shop. When they arrived, Dawson held the door open for her and she smiled at him.

"Thank you, Dawson," she said, glad to have her hands warming up in the pockets of the coat she wore. At the beginning of the pop-up performance, she had left her coat unbuttoned so her cheerful Christmas tree sweater was on display. Now, warmth was the priority.

Dawson walked in behind her. "My pleasure. Some women take offense."

"I was raised by an old-fashioned man," Marisa explained. "But I don't expect it. And I understand women who want to stand on their own. And if that includes opening their own door?" She shrugged. "Who am I to say they're wrong?"

That finally got a smile out of Dawson and that felt gratifying. How could she have missed something like his smile after only one or two days of knowing him? That was downright bizarre and inspired internal curiosity for one minute before her logical brain refocused on the task at hand—producing and directing the best darn Mistletoe Pageant show that Bronco had ever seen. A show that even the stuffy old guard would approve!

"Good morning, Mr. John." Even though the man behind the counter was much older, he spoke to Dawson in a respectful, deferential manner.

"Good morning, sir." Dawson was very polite in return, and that put a check in the column for the *things that I actually like about Dawson John* on her mental checklist.

"What can I do you for?"

"I've heard around town that you've got the best cup of hot chocolate in Bronco."

The man seemed pleased by the compliment. "I do make a mean hot chocolate. How many can I get for you?"

"Three." Dawson held up three fingers before he took his wallet out of his back pocket.

"I'm buying." Marisa pulled out her wallet too.

"Absolutely not," he argued. "It would be my pleasure."

"It would be *my* pleasure," Marisa said. "When I win today fair and square, I'll happily let you buy my dinner."

The man behind the counter delivered hot chocolates with lids on them. He'd overheard the small debate and he said, "Best just let her have her way, Mr. John. I'm a much happier man once I figured that out after twenty years of marriage."

"Thank you," Marisa said with her debit card in her hand.

"Is there anything else I can get you?" the gentleman asked. "Sticky buns, muffins, all made fresh today."

"I'd love to." Marisa put her card in the reader. "But if I

did, I would have to curl up on one of your lovely benches while I recovered from a sugar coma."

The man laughed and then handed her a receipt and asked, "Now where have I seen you before?"

She tucked her receipt into her wallet. "I'm not sure."

"This is Marisa Sanchez," Dawson said. "She's producing the Mistletoe Pageant this year."

The man thought for a moment and then snapped his fingers. "Are you any relation to Stanley Sanchez?"

"He's my great-uncle."

"Well, then, that must be it. He was in here not too long ago and showed me some videos of you singing and playing the piano." He nodded. "I knew you looked real familiar."

"I hope you will come see the show this year."

"Me and my wife, we never miss it."

Marisa and Dawson carried the cups out to where Charity was waiting for them.

"Mmm." Charity made a happy noise after her first sip. "So good."

"I agree." Marisa smiled as the hot liquid warmed her from the inside out. "It's my absolute favorite holiday indulgence."

Marisa finished her hot chocolate and then sat back down behind the keyboard. She was about to get started again when Charity spotted a friend on the other side of the park.

"I'll be right back! I haven't seen her since she left for college in August!"

"Good help," Dawson said, "is hard to find."

"A constant struggle, yes."

"I think your cold finger routine was a stall tactic. That's how I knew you're running scared," Dawson said. "Are you ready to get back to work?"

"Why are you still standing here talking smack?" Marisa stretched her fingers.

"You actually went there."

"Yes, I did," she retorted playfully. "And don't go using your good looks to sway voters to your side of the argument."

"Hey," he said, "I don't need to cheat to defeat."

Marisa began to play scales to warm up her fingers. Dawson picked up the tokens and that was when a young woman appeared on the main steps of city hall. She folded her arms tightly in front of her body in an attempt to keep warm without a coat. The woman, attractive with her blond hair styled into soft curls, waved her hands to get Dawson's attention.

"Dawson!"

He turned around, looked for the person addressing him, and then he smiled appreciatively at the well-dressed woman.

"I thought I saw you over here!" the woman said, shivering in her pencil skirt and silky blouse. "The mayor would like a quick word."

Dawson kind of shrugged before he put down the clipboard. "I'll just be a minute."

Marisa sent him a small smile and then began to play "Rudolph the Red nosed Reindeer." It was one of her absolute favorite songs all the way back to when she was a child. She had never tried to put her modern spin on this classic; it was perfect just the way it was written. As she played a small group of people began to congregate around her and, loving the energy any size audience could bring, Marisa forgot all about her cold fingers or Dawson walking off with a beautiful blonde. As she sang, the crowd grew and then she began to take requests, all the while encouraging the spectators to vote.

She was so happy, totally in her element, and having a great time catching vibes from the crowd that at first she didn't notice a police officer winding his way through the crowd until he was standing in front of her keyboard and watching her intently.

When she finished the song and after some flattering applause that also made her pretty sure she was about to win this wager, she asked the officer if everything was okay.

"Well, between you and me and this oak tree, you need to have a permit to play in the park."

"Oh!" Marisa exclaimed. "I didn't know." She was an avid rule follower! Always had been. "I'll pack up right now."

"No need. Just get a permit next time."

She didn't think there would be a next time, but she told him that she would.

"Don't stop on my account," said the officer. "I love music in the park. I think I saw you on the theater website. My wife *loves* musical theater, and she was first in line when tickets went on sale for the Mistletoe Pageant."

"I hope she will enjoy the show."

"I bet she will."

"Thanks, Officer," she said with a grateful smile.

Dawson was speaking with the mayor, Rafferty Smith, about the Mistletoe Pageant—he had heard that Charity was in the show and he wanted to know what Dawson had to say about how Marisa Sanchez was doing. Dawson only gave Marisa rave reviews and he could do it without stretching the truth. Dawson was impressed with Marisa's talent both as a musician-vocalist and a teacher. It wasn't the right moment to share his concerns about how the old guard of Bronco would respond to Marisa's take on a holiday show, especially when the focus group results hadn't been tallied.

"Thank you for your time," Mayor Smith said.

"My pleasure," Dawson replied. While he was shaking the mayor's hand, out of the corner of his eye he saw a police officer standing with Marisa.

"I'm sorry," Dawson said, "I've got something pressing to attend to."

"I understand." Rafferty nodded. "I've taken up too much of your time as it is."

Dawson left the mayor's office and rushed out of city hall, taking the steps two at a time, and running pretty darn fast in his cowboy boots over to where Marisa was talking to a police officer.

"Everything okay here?" Dawson asked.

The officer turned around, and that's when Dawson realized that the police officer was a high school buddy.

"Big D!" The officer stuck out his hand for him to shake. "How have you been?"

Dawson shook the officer's hand with a broad smile. "Good to see you, Mateo! How's the wife and kids?"

"We're good, man. Everyone's good."

"I'm glad to hear it. We're all good too." Dawson looked at Marisa. She'd stopped playing, which had caused the crowd to move away naturally. She looked upset and Dawson discovered that he didn't like how it felt to see Marisa upset. Strange times. "So, is everything okay?"

"We needed a permit," Marisa said.

"Wait a minute," the officer said to Marisa. "Is Dawson involved in this? No wonder you didn't have a permit! D has never been one for following the rules."

Marisa seemed hesitant to say one way or the other,

so Dawson quickly turned it back on himself. "Guilty as charged. If we need a citation, please make it out in my name, not in Marisa's."

Officer Lopez smiled at Dawson. "No citation. Just a friendly reminder that if you want to play in the park, get a permit first."

"Done." Dawson shook the officer's hand again.

Even though he had smoothed things over, he could see that Marisa was unhappy and she was beginning to pack up.

"I hope you aren't leaving on my account." Officer Lopez seemed genuinely concerned.

"I think it's for the best," she said. "The temperature is dropping and I can't play with my gloves on."

"Well," his high school buddy said, "would you be willing to sing one more song for my wife? She read your bio on the theater website and she even found some of your videos on TikTok." He looked over at Dawson.

Dawson was relieved to see Marisa stop packing as the lure of a fan with a favorite-song request seemed to overcome her frustration about the permit deal.

"What's your wife's favorite song?"

"Do you know 'Last Christmas' by Wham?"

And that singular question made Marisa smile and then laugh, and the happy light returned to her eyes, which made him smile too.

"I know it well!"

"Can I get this on video?" the officer asked.

Marisa said, "Of course," as she sat down on her small stool.

Just then, Charity rounded the corner, spotted the officer and then broke into a run. Winded, she asked, "What's going on? Dawson, what did you do *this* time?"

"It's okay, Charity." Marisa met Dawson's gaze after she

took him out of the hot seat with his sister. "You're just in time for Wham!"

Charity's large blue eyes lit up, her face registered sheer joy and she clasped her hands together and hopped up one time, both of her feet coming off the ground.

"Duet?" his sister asked.

"Absolutely duet!" Marisa waited for Charity to get situated and for the officer to start recording before she put her fingers to the keys.

Dawson could hear that Charity's voice blended with Marisa's in an interesting way. It was like an extra layer that captured the ear. And he wasn't the only one who liked this matchup; a new crowd was drawn to them, more votes were cast and, in the end, the officer was the last to cast a vote before leaving with his video of his wife's favorite song.

As usual, Dawson couldn't seem to take his eyes off the pretty musician. The way Marisa took Charity under her wing and worked to show her voice off while taking a supporting role really touched him. His relationship with his sister was a special one for both of them. They loved each other, they were honest with each other, they could be each other's worst critic or biggest fan. He loved everyone in his family, but everything he knew about unconditional love he'd learned from his baby sister. Even listening to Marisa perform a song that was on his *most hated* list, Dawson saw how her incredible voice cut through the human condition filled with rules and roles to reach the heart of a person. Marisa was someone very special—not just a great singer or a great musician—she was a star with a heart of gold.

"I'm tired now. Hungry and cold too," Marisa admitted. "Let's just get going."

Charity stopped her movement. "Before we know who won?"

Marisa nodded to the coffee can. "Would you like to do the honors?"

Charity dumped the chips into her hand and then counted quickly.

"Well?" he asked impatiently. "Who won?"

Charity looked at him with her best deadpan expression, building the suspense like a true performer, and then finally sang the name, "Marisa!"

Dawson frowned. "By what margin?"

"One vote." His sister grinned. "Where are you taking us for dinner?"

One of Dawson's favorite places to eat was DJ's Deluxe.

"Dawson must be trying to impress you," Charity said.

Marisa had heard of DJ's Deluxe because her cousin Camilla had worked there before opening up her own restaurant called The Library over in Bronco Valley.

"Are you sure they have seats available? It's packed," Marisa said, her stomach beginning to growl the minute she walked through the door of the upscale barbecue place. Whatever they were cooking, it smelled amazing.

"We'll get a table," Dawson said without concern.

"I don't feel like I'm dressed for this place."

"You look great," Charity was quick to say.

The hostess walked up to the podium and, just like everyone they had encountered today, Dawson was given special treatment.

"Hello, Dawson." The tall, reed-thin hostess smiled at him.

"How are you, Kirsty?"

"I'm doin' better now that you're here," the hostess said. "Will you be sittin' at the bar or do you want a table?"

Marisa's sharp, discerning eye went straight to Dawson's face but couldn't read it.

"Table. For three please."

Kirsty picked up three menus and led the way to a centrally located table. It seemed like the best table in the restaurant. Kirsty handed them all menus and said, "Enjoy your meal."

"Thank you, Kirsty."

Dawson held out a chair for his sister and turned to do the same for Marisa, but she sat down before he could. She was still feeling stunned at how Dawson had managed to get the best table after walking past a line of people that spanned the lobby and the sidewalk on the outside of the establishment.

This was supposed to be fun for all of them, so Marisa decided to let the line of questioning die out while she looked over the menu. The more she looked, the more shocked she became. She hadn't seen a menu priced like this since she'd lived in Boston for college—and on her work-study budget, she'd definitely avoided places like that back then. For Pete's sake, a simple salad was thirty dollars!

Who would pay thirty bucks for a bowl of leaves? Even if it did have some of Montana's finest goat cheese on top!

"What's wrong?" Dawson asked her.

"Nothing's wrong, really," Marisa said, and then asked, "Just as a point of clarification, are these prices for a single entrée or a whole family deal?"

Chapter Six

"I'm treating, remember?" Dawson said to her, and she appreciated his attempt to put her mind at ease. But it felt wrong to spend so much money on one meal.

Finally she decided to go with barbecue chicken and a small salad on the side.

"How is it?" Charity asked her when their meals were promptly delivered and they began to eat.

"It's so good," she said and meant it. She couldn't remember having better barbecue anywhere.

The taste of the meal didn't change how she felt: this one dinner would probably cost the same amount that her family would have spent on groceries in a week. It would've been rude to mention it, so she didn't. She did her best to enjoy the meal and put the inflated cost as much out of her mind as possible.

"So, what did you think about the focus group results?" Dawson asked her after he had wolfed down a huge premium cut steak with a side of broccoli.

Marisa put her fork down, wiped her mouth, then said, "I'm shocked, really. I thought that I would win easily. Not just by one vote."

"But you did win, Marisa," Charity reminded her. "So, I do think that Bronco is ready for some progress."

"Maybe," Marisa said, "but I need to do some rethinking though. I need to thread the new into a tapestry of tradition."

"Now, you're talking." Dawson smiled at her. "Anyone up for dessert?"

"No. No. No." Marisa shook her head. "I'm full."

"Me too," Charity agreed. "There is a part of me that would like to order a huge piece of their famous three layer Death by Chocolate cake just because I know Mom would clutch her pearls at the thought of me eating all those calories. But I'll have to give Mom apoplexy the next time."

The waitress returned and asked if anyone would like to finish the dinner with a cup of coffee.

"Yes, please," Marisa said, and then covered a yawn with her fancy napkin. "I still need to figure out how to marry tradition while still bringing my own style to the pageant. I've been thrown a curveball."

Dawson waited for the coffee to be poured before he said, "I feel like this curveball was my fault."

After adding two sugars and some cream, Marisa gratefully took a sip of the strong coffee. "I wish you wouldn't feel that way. Truly, Dawson. Yes, I have to rethink my approach, but I'm so grateful to have the time to design a show that Bronco—all parts of Bronco—will love. That's always my primary goal when producing a show like the Mistletoe Pageant. I want to create memories that will last a lifetime."

"You did win," he reminded her.

"I did," Marisa agreed. "But by a nose. I need a much wider margin if I'm going to design a show that is a success. And the only time I will truly know if I succeeded in that main goal is on opening night!"

"It's going to be great." Sweet Charity always tried to make people feel better.

"Well," Dawson leaned back, looking well-fed and happy, "I'm glad I didn't end up on your naughty list."

"Just give him time," Charity said.

That made Marisa laugh. It was so easy to be with Dawson and his sister. And she loved how they both worked overtime to make her feel comfortable in a town that, at times, felt very far away from her hometown of Tenacity.

The day in the park had tired her out and she couldn't stop yawning. "If I don't get home and get into bed, I might just embarrass the both of you by falling asleep in this chair."

They all prepared to stand up when a gentleman stopped by their table.

"Dawson John! How the heck are you?"

Dawson stood up and shook the man's hand. "DJ Traub! The man who single-handedly put Bronco on the map for our barbecue."

"How was the food tonight?" DJ asked. Marisa hadn't met the owner of DJ's Deluxe, but Camilla had talked about him often and had only positive things to say.

"Damn delicious!" Dawson sat back down. "Can you join us?"

"No," DJ said. "Not tonight. But I thank you for the offer."

"Next time, then."

"You bet." DJ nodded before he turned his attention to Charity. "Is this little Charity all grown up?"

"Hi, Mr. Traub."

"Oh, Lord, no. Mr. Traub is my father. Just DJ."

DJ walked to Marisa's side of the table and introduced himself.

"Now, didn't I see you in my Facebook feed a couple of nights back?" the owner asked her.

"Possibly. I'm Marisa Sanchez. I was interviewed about the Mistletoe Pageant by a blogger who covers all things Bronco."

"That's it. That's it. Now are you any relation to Camilla?"

"She's my cousin."

"Boy, did I hate to see her go," DJ said in a booming voice. "She was one of my best employees. But I can't stop progress. I'm glad she's got her own place now. Tell her I said hi, will you?"

Marisa nodded. "Of course I will."

"How's Thunder Canyon treating you?" Dawson asked. "And how's your family?"

DJ and his wife, Allaire, spent most of their time in their hometown of Thunder Canyon, several hundred miles away. They had another barbecue restaurant, the much more casual DJ's Rib Shack, known for its secret sauce—the recipe of which DJ still refused to reveal, even after over a decade in business.

"Right as rain," DJ said. "Right as rain."

Soon after the owner left their table, the three of them decided to head out. They all had busy days, and Marisa had so much thinking to do and she could only do that alone in a quiet space.

The minute they walked outside, a frigid gust of wind felt like pinpricks on her face. She ducked her head and walked quickly to Charity's truck.

"Drive safe," Dawson said to his sister as he held her door open.

"Yes, Dad."

Then he ushered Marisa around to the passenger side and opened the door.

"Thank you for dinner, Dawson." She held out her hand for him to shake. "And for the eye-openers." When he gripped her hand, she felt the oddly familiar warmth and excitement that only his touch seemed to induce.

"I hope to see your real soon, Marisa."

She smile at him shyly. "Me too." He shut her door, and she watched through the window as he walked to his vehicle.

Charity pulled out of the parking lot slowly. "Dawson likes you."

Marisa felt both excited and terrified. For her, she had always kept romance at bay. When she was in Boston, she kept her schedule crowded with her education and gigs with her band. Even when her fans asked her out after a gig, and some were nearly as handsome as Dawson, but no one was as handsome as Dawson, she had turned them down. When she had graduated from Berklee and returned to Tenacity, she had focused on building a career, finding ways to serve her community and making sure she contributed to her family.

She was not a naive woman, but while she had dated before, she was a novice when it came to love. Had she ever before felt this electricity light up her entire body like whenever Dawson was around? No. Not even close. While she couldn't deny it, she also didn't have time to turn this molehill into a giant mountain. Her focus was the Mistletoe Pageant; that's what needed her full attention, not some crush she had developed for one of the wealthiest, most influential, ridiculously handsome eligible bachelors of Bronco, Montana!

"I like him too." Marisa did her best to sound nonchalant.

"No," Charity said. "I mean he *really* likes you."

"You don't approve?" She could hear some defensiveness in her tone. It was an old insecurity raising its ugly head. She was confident in herself now and embraced her curves, but it hadn't always been that way.

Charity glanced over at her briefly. "Not because of you, Marisa! I would never think that! You are one of the most amazing women I've ever met. I look up to you."

"Thank you."

"God. I hate that you thought I wouldn't approve of you for my brother."

"It's been a long day for all of us. I'm tired, Charity. Don't pay any attention to me."

There was an awkward silence before Charity added, "Dawson dates around, plays the field, but hasn't really had a serious relationship yet. And he's *thirty*, right? I just don't want him to hurt you."

"He won't." Marisa said, and she felt confident in that statement. She shared undeniable chemistry with the ultra-handsome cowboy and she genuinely enjoyed his company, but she had no intention of even cracking open the door to her heart.

"I hope not," Charity said uncertainly. "I've never seen him like this before. The way he looks at you. The way he is so concerned about you…"

"I'll be okay." She did her best to reassure her young protégé. "I have three weeks to launch this show. I have to focus on that."

Charity dropped her off at her car, which she had left in the theater parking lot.

"Text me when you get home?" Charity asked her.

"I will." Marisa shut the passenger door. "Get some rest. We have a long day tomorrow."

* * *

"Who the heck told you all of that?" Dawson asked his brothers Jameson and Maddox.

"Dad told us, but I don't know which part of the grapevine got ahold of his ear," Maddox said, holding the board in place while Dawson hammered a nail long enough to hold the wood in place.

Fixing fences was something the John brothers did together that allowed them to catch up without interruption.

"That means Mom knows," Dawson said.

"I don't think so," Jameson said. "Dad doesn't want to be bothered, and if he thinks Mom will chew on his ear for several hours, that's strong motivation to keep his mouth shut."

"I agree," Maddox said. "So what part of the gossip is true?"

Dawson grabbed a thermos of water, took a long draw out of it and then handed it to Maddox. "A fraction as usual. I didn't have to stop Charity from getting arrested, I didn't get into a fight with a police officer, I didn't make out with the mayor's secretary and I didn't take two women out on a date. Yes, I took two women out to dinner but Charity was one of them!"

"Is that Marisa sitting with you at the table?" Maddox asked.

"Her name is Marisa Sanchez," Dawson said, annoyed. "And yes, she was there."

The brothers moved to the next part of the fence that needed mending, and Dawson wished that he could steer the conversation away from Marisa entirely. He felt out of his depth with her—she always managed to find something that put him in a negative light, and he was beginning to think her reciprocating his sincere feelings for her was a total impossibility. Even the reserved table had been a point of contention. He'd taken many women to DJ's Deluxe, and not one of them had ever complained about the reserved table or the prices on the menu. He had hoped to impress Marisa, and that had backfired on him pretty epically. He had hoped that a day out on the range with his brothers would be a way for him to lick his wounds in peace. But all his brothers seemed to want to talk about was Marisa.

"So who is this girl to you?" Jameson asked.

"She's closer to thirty, so 'girl' doesn't really apply."

Jameson looked up at him, hammer in hand, and after a second said, "You've got it bad, little brother."

"Why? Because I don't think you should refer to her as a girl when she is clearly a grown-ass woman?"

"Yeah." Jameson went back to his work. "That's the sum of it."

Dawson lifted up a board from the trailer hooked to their ranch truck and carried it over to Maddox.

"A *woman* from Tenacity isn't going to get by Mimi," Jameson added.

"Well, I wish you good luck, little brother." Jameson stood upright to take the pressure off his back. "I want you to be happy, and if this Marisa does it for you, I'll stand right there beside you."

"Second that," Maddox said.

"Well, I don't think it's going to come to that," Dawson told them. "She doesn't feel that way about me."

Maddox looked at him disbelievingly. "That can't be right. What put that into your head?"

Dawson went back to the trailer for another board. "She's different from anyone I've ever met. She's more interested in giving back to people in her community than going out on expensive dates. She almost lost her mind over the prices at DJ's Deluxe."

"She sounds like a departure for you," said Maddox, "Not the obvious choice."

"She is different," he agreed. "A once in a lifetime kind of woman."

Maddox and Jameson exchanged a look before his oldest brother asked, "Does she think you're a once in a lifetime man?"

"Damned if I know! She thinks the special treatment I get because of our last name is a mark against me! Like last night, there was a line and we go to jump the line and got seated quickly at one of the best tables. Now there isn't anything I can do about that, now, can I?"

"Not a thing," Maddox agreed. "You didn't choose the family you were born into."

Dawson said, "I only have three weeks to show her that we can make it work with us."

"How do you know it will?" Jameson asked.

"Gut feeling," Dawson said.

Jameson hammered in a nail and then took a break long enough to ask, "Do you want a piece of advice?"

"Not really." Dawson had now grown tired of the conversation. Nothing his brothers could say would stop his heart from aching. He wanted to impress Marisa, prove that he was worthy, but all of his old tools in his "romance the ladies" toolbox didn't really work all that well on Marisa. Maybe his brothers were right; maybe his feelings for Marisa were doomed to cause him pain. But that didn't change how he felt about her.

"Well, you're gonna get it anyhow because it's my job to look out for you," Jameson told him. "Whatever you think you feel for this woman—"

"Marisa…"

"Rethink it real quick." Jameson continued, "She's not going to pass muster with Randall and Mimi. That's the real bottom line. And *if* what you're telling us is true—that you truly do care for Marisa—then you'd be selfish to put her through it. Unless you're absolutely sure she can stand up to the pressure. If you're not one hundred percent on that…" He shrugged. "Then maybe Maddox is right. Go fish in a more acceptable pond."

Dawson had respected Jameson as the eldest of the siblings, but today more than any other day in recent memory, he wanted to punch Jameson right between the eyes.

Dawson spent time mulling over what his brothers had said to him. Was he being selfish in this compulsion that was driving him to seek Marisa out? It certainly hadn't been planned. When he had driven Charity to her audition, he couldn't have known that he would meet a woman who had changed him so profoundly on the inside. Yes, of course, there were differences between them, but why did that have to be a deal-breaker? There were plenty of marriages between couples who were polar opposites. So after a full day of thinking about his predicament, Dawson decided to call Marisa just to check on her.

She answered the phone on the second ring. "Hi, Dawson."

"Hi, Marisa." His heart had begun to race with excitement at the mere sound of her melodic voice. "How are you How'd it go today?"

Dawson had checked with Charity that rehearsals had concluded for the day, and he had planned his phone call accordingly.

Marisa let out a long sigh, and that told him everything he needed to know without her saying it.

"Would you like to talk about it?" he asked as gently as he could.

"Well," Marisa said, "the focus group…"

Dawson cursed silently—he knew he had really screwed things up with that suggestion. At that point, he had been interested in finding a plausible reason to spend time with Marisa, but he also knew that he wanted her to consider how the old guard might feel about the major changes she had made to a dearly held, time-honored tradition of the Mistletoe holiday pageant. Ever since he was a little boy, his family attended the holiday show and then followed that up with a family trip to the Mistletoe Rodeo. In fact, all of the John siblings had participated in the rodeo over the years.

"I feel real bad that I talked you into that stupid focus group," Dawson told her. "I can tell you have had some time to think it over and you don't sound happy."

"I have. And I wish you'd stop blaming yourself. Was it the result I expected? No. But it's reality and I have to make some tough decisions to pivot back to a more traditional show. It'll take time and I don't have a whole lot of that."

He said, "I feel like I've got to do something to make amends here, Marisa. What can I do?"

There was a long silence on the other end of the line, followed by another heavy sigh, before she said, "Thank you, truly. But some things I just have to figure out on my own."

"Just talk to me," he prompted her. "I'm a great sounding board."

He hadn't meant to make her laugh, but he was still glad he did.

"I don't really see you as the sounding board type."

"Well," he said, "just goes to show you that you can't judge a book by its cover, now, can you?"

"I suppose not," she said. "I'm still trying to figure out how to take the feedback from the focus group and change the show accordingly. I guess I really thought I'd win everyone over a hundred percent and have no holdouts."

He waited for her to continue, grateful that she was talking through her thoughts with him. It kept her on the line and it kept her connected to him and that's what he wanted: to help and to stay connected.

"My problem is that once I have a vision set in my mind, I can be quite rigid about it. And that makes it difficult for me to change it last minute."

"I shouldn't have talked you into that focus group idea," he repeated.

This time she addressed that concern. "Dawson, no, of course I don't like to hear that some people aren't wild about my plan for the show. But I'm grateful that you helped me figure out a way to understand what people are thinking and feeling and how I can make adjustments. My dilemma now is that I need to manage to stay true to myself, honor the reason I was hired in the first place, while meeting Bronco where it is now."

"What can I do, Marisa?" he asked again. "I want to help."

"I feel like I'm on the verge of a breakthrough that would allow me to take the pulse of Bronco as a whole, to experience it in a way that would shine a spotlight on the path forward."

After a minute of racing through possible scenarios to help Marisa, Dawson asked, "How about this idea? How about we return to the scene of the crime?"

"Do you mean, Permit-Gate?"

Dawson laughed. The fact that Marisa could make him laugh whenever he spoke to her was a powerful drug.

"Yes," he said with good humor in his voice.

"Not that I doubt your sincerity, Dawson. But how would going back there help me? I feel like I understand that the old guard wants to hold on to tradition. I've run up against this at times in Tenacity, and I'm one of their own!"

"No," he disagreed. "I don't think you have, honestly. I'd like to describe Bronco as it will be during the first week of December."

"I don't think so… I feel like I've playing hooky too much with you because you're fun to hang out with."

"Thank you. You're fun too. Can you trust me on this, Marisa? I believe in my gut that this is what you need. I can paint the scene for you and show you pictures that I've taken over the years."

When she didn't respond, he asked, "What do you think? Meet me at Bronco Java and Juice tomorrow after rehearsals?"

"Okay," she finally said. "Maybe it won't help but it doesn't hurt to try."

Chapter Seven

The next day, Marisa had found it very difficult to focus on rehearsals when she knew that she would be seeing Dawson at the end of her day. She couldn't change her growing feelings for the handsome Bronco cowboy—that was the stuff of the heart—but she did recognize that, even if they did have a sweet and spicy holiday romance, it could only be *that*. Using her mother's own recipe, Marisa *was* happier when Dawson was around, she did miss him when he was away, but she could not see him in her future in the one-horse town of Tenacity.

The man she imagined who would eventually be her husband didn't have a face, but he did have traits and qualities that had always been nonnegotiable—humble, hardworking and willing to share her passion for community service. She had to give back to Tenacity! What would she have turned out to be without the support of her community? Even the plane ticket that flew her to start her college career at Berklee was paid for from a collection plate that had been passed around in their church. It wasn't his fault really, but Dawson could never understand what it felt like to do without. He could never understand what it felt like to have an entire community rally to lift up one of their

own so she could succeed. And, while he could never understand it, she knew that she could never forget it.

"Hi there." Dawson had arrived before her and had
seemed to be standing by the front door of Bronco Java
and Juice so he could open it for her.

"Hi, Dawson," she said, with that same, wonderful,
warm and tingly feeling that swept over her body whenever he was near her.

She walked in, pulled off her gloves and hat, and then
Dawson was there to help her take off her overcoat. Underneath her dark blue conservative long coat, she had donned
one of her favorite ugly holiday sweaters that portrayed the
first Christmas flight of Rudolph the Red-Nosed Reindeer.
Her favorite part of this sweater was the fact that Rudolph's
red nose actually blinked.

"That's a nice sweater."

"Why thank you, Dawson. Would you like to borrow
it sometime?"

"Super tempting." Dawson smiled at her. "You love
Christmas, don't you?"

"What tipped you off?" She returned his smile.

"Wild guess."

Together they walked up to the counter and he ordered
coffee for himself and then looked at her before he said, "One
large hot chocolate, with extra marshmallows, right?" At
her nod, he added, "Go grab a seat and I'll meet you there."

While she waited for him, she tried very hard not to stare
at him. How could a human be that perfectly made? Dawson walked with the confidence of a man who had been
given every physical advantage. His features were strong,
symmetrical, from his jawline to the dimple in the chin to
the firm shape of his lips. A sonnet could be written about
the kissability of Dawson John's lips. The man should be in

Hollywood making blockbuster movies to give the women of the world something to fantasize about this holiday season, not ordering a hot chocolate for her.

"Sorry," he said, "no marshmallows today."

"It's okay. Thank you," she said, when he joined her at the table and handed her the cup. She blew on the hot chocolate to cool it off but she just couldn't wait, so she took a sip and promptly burned her lips and the roof of her mouth.

"I'll never learn," she said.

"Burn your mouth?"

"Absolutely I did."

"Was it worth it?"

"Absolutely it was."

"Well, just in case they were out," Dawson said, tugging a small bag out of his shirt pocket. "Perhaps this will help cool it off."

"Dawson John! Are you ridiculously handsome *and* sweet?"

Dawson flashed her that winning smile with a wink and a look in his eye that set every bell and whistle in her body.

As Marisa watched Dawson fill her cup, she felt like her love-meter siren was blasting in her ears. Had any man been so attentive to what made her happy? Yes, she had been pursued back in her college days, but it had been easy for her to resist their often half-hearted attempts. There was nothing half-hearted about Dawson's gestures toward her. The man carried a baggie of mini marshmallows in his shirt pocket just so he could, in her mind, see the smile that it brought to her face.

"How is it?" he asked.

"Perfect now," she said, then asked, "So, I'm assuming you do have a job other than providing me with marshmallows and helping me understand Bronco better."

Dawson laughed. Just yesterday his brothers had been complaining about his recent absences from their ranch work. "I admit I've been playing hooky with you, but my brothers owe me some from their days when they were romancing soon-to-be wives."

Marisa's heart felt like it skipped a bit when Dawson mentioned "wives" as it related to him playing the same kind of "love" hooky. Did Dawson think of her in that way? As a wife? They hadn't even had a first real date unless coffee at the Eat, Gas, Go counted.

After they finished their drinks, they both put on their winter gear. He held the door open for her, and she walked out into the chilly November day. They walked together across the street to the park where she had won their bet by one vote. She wasn't a whiz at statistics but that margin could not be viewed as significant. For all intents and purposes, it was a tie.

On the way across the street, Marisa's foot hit a slick patch of ice and as her foot slid forward, tipping her off balance, she reached for the only thing sturdy enough to stop her from falling.

Holding on to Dawson's arm, Marisa fought to steady herself. He stopped walking, put his hand under her elbow and helped her to stand upright.

"Better?" he asked.

"Yes," Marisa said, annoyed that she had just played a damsel in distress with Dawson coming to her rescue.

She had to stop focusing on Dawson's handsomeness, the woodsy scent of his skin and the way he looked at her with those ocean-blue eyes, making her want to spend all day just swimming in them. She was here on a mission to save the Mistletoe Pageant, *not* to ogle a cowboy.

Dawson looked over at her, seemed to be about to say

something to her when he slipped on an icy patch in his fancy cowboy boots. She reached out to break his fall, which was a fool's errand in the light of the fact that he was much taller and his body was heavy from tightly packed muscles.

Somehow, Dawson managed to stop his fall while not pulling her down. After a quick minute, he said, "We appear to be having some difficulty walking today."

Marisa, as she often did with Dawson, laughed happily. "What's wrong with us today?"

Dawson met her gaze and for the briefest of moments, he let her see what was hidden behind his incredible eyes and, on a soul level, she knew exactly what he was feeling because she was feeling it too.

Chemistry.

Undeniable attraction.

Even possibly, love.

She was conscious of the fact that Bronco, while not as tiny as Tenacity, was still small enough for the gossip mill to be fully operational. No matter what romantic notions she was having for Dawson John, Marisa was keenly aware of the fact that he was the son of a highly influential family. From her experience, she wouldn't be his family's first choice in the love department, and it was impossible for her to imagine Dawson getting the green light from her father or her brothers.

"I'm ready to be inspired," she told Dawson, clinging to a tiny ray of hope that he could help her break through her creative block. "Are you the ghost of Christmas past, present or future top help me see the errors of my modern musical theater ways?"

"I think you've got a handle on the present..."

"Maybe."

"And I'm not psychic, so I've got no business trying to make any predictions."

"Except to tell me that my show, as it stands right now, might draw the wrath of the old guard and cause a boycott of the Mistletoe Pageant!"

Dawson frowned at her. "I did make that prediction, didn't I?"

"That would be a yes, Dawson. But… I think that you can predict the future. There have already been some complaints on the theater website."

"That was lightning quick even by Bronco standards."

"Maybe Bronco doesn't want a stranger to run a historical event."

"Well, I'm not happy to be right about that," he said, and then tried to lighten the mood. "So, I'll be your ghost of Bronco Christmas past…"

"Eeeeew," she teased him, and he was glad she was willing to follow him back to their playful mood. "Spooky!"

Dawson felt as if he'd never truly known what it meant to be happy. He had never expected any woman, or any one person, to make him happy—he knew that this was his job to do. But when he was with Marisa, he recognized that pre-Marisa, he hadn't drilled down to his soul, hadn't uncovered what could make him feel satisfied, content, filled to the brim with joy. Post-Marisa…he knew it exactly. He was certain what he felt for her was love. Plain, simple love. Now that didn't mean that a relationship with Marisa would be plain or simple. As much as he professed his "I don't care" attitude when he was talking with his brothers, there was a very real part of him that wanted his parents to approve of his choice and embrace the woman he intended to marry.

Could that ever happen if his chosen was Marisa San-chez who would be a wonderful daughter-in-law but didn't come from a cattle baron family? Dawson answered his question with a small shake of his head before he shut down that part of his brain and focused his attention on helping Marisa. At the most basic level, he had discovered Marisa wanted Bronco to love her version of the Mistletoe Pageant.

Dawson pulled up some pictures he had taken at the tree lighting ceremony the year before.

Marisa studied the pictures and then looked at the un-decorated park before her. "So, the tree goes right there?"

"Yes," he said. "Tree lighting always happens on the first Saturday in December. The streets are lined with vendors and performers—"

"All with permits," she interjected with good humor.

"Yes." He laughed. "Most certainly."

"Tell me more," she urged him, and he enjoyed watching her as she worked through her creative process, certain he had never met, and would never meet, a woman who was as gifted as Marisa. She was a genius; he was convinced of it. And admitting that to himself exposed a fault-line crack in his rock-solid self-esteem. Was he good enough for a woman like Marisa? There wasn't a frivolous bone in her body; quite the opposite in fact. She was incredibly focused and determined, and she was driven by a deep de-sire to serve.

They sat down on a nearby bench while he painted a pic-ture of the idyllic Bronco holiday cheer. Every streetlamp, every traffic light, every window in the historic Bronco City Hall building would be dressed with lights and garland and wreaths. Kids would be entertained by face painting and ornament decorating, and bursting with energy from too many cups of hot chocolate. A modern touch had been added, Dawson told her—the many selfie stations replete with holiday cutouts.

"It all sounds so…" She paused, seeming to look for the right words. "Perfect."

"For us here in Bronco, that month leading into the new year is something that we look forward."

"Even cowboys like you?" she said quietly.

"Even cowboys like me," he agreed. "Maybe especially cowboys like me."

"How so?" She looked at him suspiciously and teased, "Are you a spy for the old guard?"

"You never know," he said. He winked at her, enjoying the feel of her body innocently resting next to his on the bench. "John men aren't raised to be emotional."

"But you love the traditions just as I love mine in Tenacity. I also love the excitement of creating something new—something that could become one of those traditions over the years."

"I think that describes me too." Dawson met her gaze. "And when I was a boy, I could just be a boy when my family came to this park. I didn't have to worry about being tough or the best this or that. I could just be…"

"You," she said. "No strings attached."

"Right."

After some thought, Marisa said, "I think that I've been so determined to fulfill the order, I guess I can put it like that, of the why I was hired in the first place. If my video hadn't gone viral, I wouldn't be sitting here on this bench with you right now. I would be back in my safe playground in Tenacity, where most of my ideas, no matter how outside of the box, are embraced by my community even if they don't like them."

"I think that's right."

"That's what you've been trying to show me."

"I feel like I didn't show it to you in the right way," he said. "And I'm sorry for that."

She turned toward him, touched his arm and said, "You showed me in the best way, Dawson. I don't know how you *knew* what I needed but you did know."

He put his hand over her mittened hand. "Then, I'm glad I could help."

Marisa turned her body forward but left her hand on his arm for a couple of moments longer. He fought the urge to reach for it, to hold on to that hand for the rest of his natural born days. But his brother's warnings worked on his mind, twisted things up for him, so he didn't act on impulse. Instead, he told himself to enjoy Marisa in this moment and let destiny work out some of the parts that seemed impossible between them.

"The memories you have of Christmas here in Bronco are close to my own memories of the holiday season in Tenacity."

Dawson listened to her, wanting her to talk more so he could always have the memory of her silky, smooth voice burned in his brain.

"My parents didn't have a lot of money. There were five of us kids, so that's a lot of mouths to feed."

"Christmas must have been incredibly difficult for my parents. They always wanted us to have everything that we wanted, but they couldn't provide it. I believe, even though they've never said it and I've never asked, that this caused my parents deep pain that they carry even to this day."

"What traditions did you have growing up?" he asked.

Marisa smiled. "We had wonderful traditions. Even though there wasn't money for all of those store-bought things that we wanted, and I can only speak for myself,

I always remember our Christmas Eve and day being the best days of the year. My mom would make us all matching pajamas. She even made a pair for our dad."

"And he wore them?"

"He did." Marisa recalled the holidays with a bright smile. "He was and still is such a strong man—a man among men—but for us and for his wife, Will Sanchez put on those pajamas and wore them with pride."

"Sounds like a man I'd like to know."

Marisa looked up into his face and he could see his comment about her father had struck a chord in her. "He is a wonderful man. His whole purpose in life is to take care of his family. That's what drives him."

"We always watched *It's a Wonderful Life* while we trimmed the tree. My parents had some ornaments from their childhood—a wooden sleigh carved by my father's grandfather and my mom had a small handmade doll that her mother had made for her. The doll looked just like my mom and had a matching Christmas dress. And, of course, mom and dad hung up every handmade ornaments us kids made. Each year, they get more and more tattered and we beg her to throw them away, but she just puts a little tape over the rips and hangs them for another year."

"I like the sound of your family Christmas."

"It's always seemed so magical to me. I want to carry on these traditions with my own family one day." In the short time they had spent together, marriage and family had come up several times. Other women had brought up the subject, hinting about marriage and or a long term commitment but he let that topic die as soon as it was raised. It was different with Marisa. The topic of family, kids, marriage were not shut down on his end and he could see Marisa as a wonderful mother as she continued her description of her family traditions. "When we were little kids, we always tried to wait up for Santa but we never could. I remember falling asleep on the couch with my siblings and then waking up in my own bed, bright and early on Christmas morning. While Dad was filling up on homemade Christmas cookies and milk, he must have carried us, one by one, to our beds."

"It sounds like you have a close family."

She nodded. "I do. We were always rich in love."

"I admire that."

Marisa had an odd look in her eyes when she looked up at him, but the thoughts behind that expression weren't vocalized.

"I'm close with my brothers," Dawson said.

"And your sister."

He nodded his agreement. "My folks are a different breed really. Too much keeping up with the Joneses and not enough enjoying what we have right now."

"They can't be all that bad. You seemed to have turned out all right, and Charity is one of the sweetest people I've ever met in my life."

"Charity is the crown jewel of the family, I'll give you that. But us John siblings made a concerted effort to go down the exact opposite path than the one our parents set up for us. In my mind, life's too darn short to spend so much time worrying about what other people think. But they're my parents and I love them."

"We don't always agree with our parents. I think it would be odd if we did." Marisa said to him kindly, "I see you with your sister and I know what kind of man you are on the inside. A family man."

As if the universe had given them a perfect chance to get their focus back on Christmas Bronco style, big, fat, snow flakes began top fall from the sky.

Marisa held out her gloved hands to catch snowflakes that had begun to fall. "It's snowing!"

The falling snowflakes grabbed his companion's attention, and Dawson was glad for it.

Marisa spun around in a circle, head back, arms outstretched as she tried to catch the fluffy snowflakes on her tongue.

"Isn't this just the most magical time of the year, Dawson? In just a few weeks, it'll be Thanksgiving."

"Of course," He smiled at her as he enjoyed her ability to be perfectly in the moment.

Dawson acted on sheer instinct, not giving it much thought at all when he took her into his arms, in broad daylight, in one of the most traversed parts of town, and spun her around in a circle before letting her twirl under his arm. After several fast twirls, Marisa laughed and told him that she was dizzy. He stopped twirling her and then held her close to his body until the dizziness subsided.

"I love to twirl!" Marisa stepped back once she was seeing clearly.

He almost let it slip—it was right there on the tip of his tongue. *I love you.* Three simple words he had never said to anyone other than his relatives. I. Love. You.

"Thank you for this, Dawson," she said after he walked her to her car. "It's exactly what I needed."

"Then I'm glad," he said, his hands on her driver's-side door. "I like spending time with you."

"I like spending time with you," Marisa said unexpectedly.

"Maybe we could spend some more time together while you're still here in Bronco."

"This weekend I'm letting everyone off from rehearsal," she told him.

"What would you like to do?"

"Well, I like to dance," she told him.

"As you wish."

Dawson shut her door and watched her pull out and drive away. He had just secured an official date with the pretty pageant director. How would he manage to keep her at a safe distance when all he wanted to do was take her into his arms, kiss her like she'd never been kissed before in her life, and hold her close for the rest of their days. He didn't know how he would do it, but if he loved her, and he truly felt that he did, then the best thing he could do was let her go. He couldn't stand the idea of his lovely Marisa ever being on the receiving end of Randall and Mimi's disapproval. Now that he was certain that he had fallen in love with Marisa, her happiness outweighed his own. At the end of this, he had to let her go, and he would let her go. In the meantime, he wanted to make as many memories with Marisa as he could, and he would hold those memories close in his heart for the rest of his days on this Earth. Of that, he was certain.

"So, what do you think?" Marisa asked Charity.

It was the end of their last rehearsal before the weekend they would be off for rest and reenergizing before the major push to opening night.

Charity, as always, was the last one to leave the theater, helping her pack up for the night. "I think it's a perfect blend between Bronco's traditional soul while moving the dial just a smidge in the direction of newfangled tunes that will lead to our ruination." Her voice carried a teasing tone.

Marisa shook her head. "That was eerily descriptive."

Charity laughed good-naturedly. "Oh, Marisa, relax! I

was totally kidding. My prediction? You are going to be the toast of the town!"

As they walked out of the theater together, Charity said, "I'm kind of shocked that Dawson helped you figure things out. I wouldn't have cast him for that role."

Marisa couldn't help but smile; without saying it directly, Dawson's sister had just told her that her brother was behaving out of character. It made her feel special, and she had given up trying to lie to herself about her deepening feelings for the cowboy.

"He's taking me out dancing." Marisa felt close enough with Charity to give up that secret.

Charity titled her head to the side when she heard that news. "A real date?"

"I suppose." Marisa shrugged. "I…like him."

"He likes you too," Charity said easily. "I wasn't okay with it in the beginning."

Those words felt like a deep cut. "You didn't approve of me for him?"

Charity's lovely features crumpled as she reached out to touch her arm. "Marisa, no! That's not what I meant at all! Please believe me! I love Dawson. Always have, always will. But I didn't think he was the right one for you, not the other way around."

"Oh." That was the only thing she could think to say.

Charity shrugged one shoulder. "So I've given it long deliberation and I've come to a decision." The frown she wore turned into a brilliant grin. "I'm going to give him one chance with you."

Chapter Eight

Marisa took extra care with her outfit, her makeup and her hair. It was Friday night, and Dawson would be meeting her at the theater where he would take them both to a place called Wild Willa's Saloon. She had decided to leave her ugly Christmas sweaters in the drawer and put on one of her sassy Rank 45 rodeo button-down shirts in a maroon-red that showed off her black hair and dark brown eyes in their best light. She didn't typically wear makeup but did use a sparing amount for her date with Dawson. The mascara made her eyelashes look thick and long and hopefully it would draw Dawson's attention to her instead of any other women who would be at the bar.

"Where are you off to looking so pretty?" Her great-uncle Stanley stopped by the bathroom on his way to his own bedroom.

"I'm going to go kick my heels up a bit," she told him. It was the truth if not the whole truth.

She wasn't sure that she wanted her family to know about her budding friendship/relationship with Dawson. Besides, her great-uncle was already sad enough. After losing his wife of sixty years, the family had convinced him to leave his life in Mexico to start anew in Bronco, Montana. It wasn't long before lightning had struck Stanley twice and he fell in love with the elderly, free-spirited town psychic Winona Cobbs and proposed. Everyone believed that Stanley and Winona would enjoy a short courtship before they tied the knot. But when Winona disappeared on their wedding day without saying a word, Stanley experienced his second heartbreak. The entire Bronco Sanchez family tried their best to support him while he figured out what had happened to his beloved bride-to-be.

"Good girl," Stanley said, his shoulders drooped forward. "You deserve it. You've got the strong Sanchez work ethic."

Marisa hugged Stanley. "Thank you. That means a lot to me coming from you."

Stanley held on to her a while longer before he shuffled down the hall. Then, he stopped and turned back to her. "If you ever find love, *mi sobrina*, hold on to it real tight and don't ever let it go."

"I will, *tio*." She promised him, wishing that he could find Winona.

Not wanting to explain herself to anyone else in the small, cozy house, Marisa grabbed her car keys and coat and slipped out quietly into the frigid winter air, feeling like a teenager sneaking out of the house for the first time.

She drove the short distance to the theater and felt relieved when she saw that Dawson had beaten her to it. She parked next to his massive GMC truck, and he was there to open the door and hold out his hand for her to take as she got out from behind the wheel.

"Cold enough for you?" Dawson asked.

"I've got Montana blood running through my veins, same as you, don't forget," she bantered. "This is beach weather."

"You look mighty pretty, Ms. Sanchez."

He offered her his arm and for the first time, she took it. Why pretend that she wasn't interested? Why pretend that she didn't want to be next to him? As far as she could tell, the feeling was mutual.

"I was just thinking the same thing about you!" She felt giddy like she had just had two glasses of pink champagne.

Marisa climbed up into the passenger seat of Dawson's truck, then he shut the door before he walked quickly around the truck to join her in the cab.

"Are you ready for a good time?" Dawson asked her.

"You have no idea."

Dawson drove them to the Wild Willa's Saloon while she told him about the changes in the show she'd decided on following the focus group and the walk down Bronco Park Christmas memory lane.

"So far, things are going rather smoothly. I met with the band earlier today, and they're really nailing the jazzed-up versions that I'm keeping in the show, and the dances are starting to come together…"

"And Charity?"

"She is my best performer. Such a quick study. I really can't imagine the show without her."

Dawson pulled into the crowded parking lot; they weren't the only ones who were looking for a good time. It had been such a long time since she had gone on a date that she began to have a severe case of anxiety. She was stepping out with Dawson John, and it struck her as a potentially horrible idea.

"Wild Willa's Saloon." Dawson shut off the engine. "Home of the Get Lucky Bar, the one and only bar that is shaped like a four-leaf clover."

"It looks crowded."

"Friday night."

Marisa wanted to find a way to back out of the date; she was fairly well-known around town because she had been in the newspaper and on the local news, and Dawson was Bronco elite and it seemed like everyone knew him. What if Bronco didn't like the idea of her dating one of their favorite sons? Could this one night unravel all of the work she'd done on the show to fit the town's expectations?

While Dawson walked around to her side of the truck, Marisa truly contemplated backing out. But the brief exchange with her great-uncle Stanley, so sad and downtrodden while he mourned the loss of his beloved Winona, smacked her right in the forehead. She knew what he was saying to her—don't forgo love for work.

Dawson opened her door, held out his hand and asked, "Ready?"

"Yes, I am." She took his offered hand. "More than ready, I think."

Dawson felt proud to have Marisa on his arm as they entered one of his favorite watering holes. He was certain that he'd run into plenty of people he knew; he was taking Marisa to a place that would put a spotlight on them. But he didn't care. He only wanted to make Marisa happy, to show her a good time, to enjoy each other.

No doubt they were going to run into women he'd dated casually over the years and friends that he'd grown up with. And all of them were going to be curious when they saw him with a woman who was nearly the exact opposite of his so-called "type." But over the last couple of weeks he figured out that the women he'd been dating weren't actually his type. Marisa was. But how could he have known it without first meeting her?

"You want a drink?" he asked her.

"Sure," she said. "I'll take a beer."

"Tap or bottle?"

"Bottle."

Dawson ordered two bottles of beer for them before he led the way through the crowd to find an empty booth near the dance floor that was situated in the center of the four-leaf clover.

"Here's to an excellent Mistletoe Pageant." He held out his bottle for her to clink.

"Here's hoping." She took a swig of her beer and then said, "This place is cool."

"I've always thought so," he said, avoiding the eye of a couple of women he had dated a couple of times.

"Hey!" Marisa exclaimed. "That's my band!"

The local band that had been working with Marisa on the pageant walked from the bar and began setting up their instruments.

"Live music Friday nights," he said.

"I'm going to go say hi to them."

Dawson watched Marisa walk over to the small stage, and he had to admit that he liked what he saw of her coming and going. She was petite with an hourglass figure that he had learned to appreciate. She wore slender fit jeans that hugged her in all of the right places. He would be a liar if he hadn't tried to imagine what it would be like to hold her in his arms, skin to skin. And he wasn't the only one in the bar appreciating the view as she walked in a confident, head-held-high gait, a lovely swing in her hips. He caught several men admiring her, and he didn't feel threatened at all—he knew that if Marisa came with him, she would leave with him. And he felt completely secure in that knowledge.

"Hey, man." One of his friends from high school stopped at the booth.

"Hey, Sam." Dawson stood up, shook hands and then sat back down. "Good to see you."

"Did I see you come in with Marisa?" Sam took a seat. "You did."

"I've been working on building some sets for her," his old friend said. "You've got a tiger by the tail with that one."

That made Dawson laugh and relax some. Sam Scott was a good guy—nonjudgmental. They had been fierce rivals during their high school football years and had managed to become friends after they had graduated. They shared a passion for the outdoors, fast cars and any sport that got the blood and adrenaline pumping.

Marisa came bouncing up to the booth, her eyes shining and a broad smile on her face that only served to endear her to him more.

"Sam!" she said. "Aren't you supposed to be working on my set?"

"Just takin' a little break." Sam stood up, gave her a friendly hug, and then let Dawson have his time with Marisa.

"I didn't know you knew Sam." She took another swig of her beer.

"Since high school."

"He's pretty amazing. I've worked with a lot of carpenters, but he's a genius when it comes to woodwork. I'm thinking of asking him to come to Tenacity to refresh some of stage props for our Christmas show."

"Should I be worried?" he asked, teasing.

She gave one shoulder a shrug. "Only when it comes to woodwork."

The band finished setting up and then the relatively empty dance floor became crowded. Marisa finished off her beer and then jumped up to join the line dancing that had just started. Sometimes he forgot that, at her core, she was a down-home Montana country girl. Marisa knew all of the line dances from the Cowboy Cha Cha to the Tush Push. At first Marisa started in the back row but worked her way right up to the front row. Next thing he knew, Marisa was giving some of the novices a tutorial.

Dawson did the right thing and ordered them another round of beer. After all of that dancing, Marisa would be parched. After another tutorial to Double D, Marisa headed his way, her face glistening with sweat, her face beaming with joy.

"Wow!" She sat down across from him. "I can't remember having more fun! This is exactly what I needed."

"Happy to oblige."

"How do you always know what I need?" She asked him a pointed question, but he didn't know the answer. Lately, he'd managed to do the right thing with her; he didn't want to press his luck too much, even though they were currently sitting in the Get Lucky Bar.

"Don't you want to dance?" she asked before he could reply.

"I'll wait until we get to the couples dances. Then I'll show you all of my moves, little lady." He gave her a wink. "So far, I've had a good time just watching you."

Her face was rosy from dancing, but he thought he saw an extra blush on her cheeks.

"You are beautiful, Marisa."

She ducked her head, the first sign of shyness she had exhibited that evening. Then, she glanced up at him and said, "And you're very handsome, Dawson. But I have to imagine you know that already."

He leaned forward, reached for her hand and told her, "Everything matters more when I hear it from you."

Dawson saw the surprise alight in her eyes, and he saw her process his words and then meet his gaze straight on. He had just opened the door for her to see what was in his heart and what was in his soul. She couldn't mistake his feelings for her after that. Surely she couldn't.

"You aren't what I expected," she said.

In that moment, Dawson felt like the world had faded to black, and only the two of them existed in the small space of the booth.

"You weren't what I expected either."

There was a long silence between them, and he wondered if they had both said too much for an evening that was supposed to be lighthearted and fun. That's when the band came to their rescue, moving on from line dancing to swing dancing. This was the perfect chance to get Marisa into his arms and keep her there for a good long while.

"Are you ready to be impressed?" he asked.

"Show me what you've got, cowboy."

Ever since she had arrived in Bronco, Marisa had felt hemmed in, under a microscope, and worried about every move she made. No, she had never been a party girl—she had always provided the entertainment. But she had literally and figuratively let her hair down at Wild Willa's Saloon! If she had to analyze it, she felt comfortable with Dawson. She felt accepted by this man in a way she had only felt with family and close friends in Tenacity.

"I've got to give you credit," she said as Dawson whirled her around the dance floor. "You know your way around a dance floor."

Dawson pulled her closer and held on to her tightly as if he were afraid she would vanish into thin air. When her big, strong, strapping cowboy had to take a break from dancing, she found her way to the microphone onstage. When she had said hello to the band, they had asked her to sing with them. Dancing with Dawson had truly been the highlight of the evening, but singing onstage was a very close second.

"A very good friend of mine requested this song," Marisa said. "So, Dawson, this one's for you."

Marisa counted off the beat and then she began to sing "Ask Me How I Know" by Garth Brooks. If there was a message for her in these lyrics, she didn't want to ask. This budding romance would be a shooting star, fast and brilliant but gone too quickly leaving only a trace of light in its wake.

She sang several more songs before the four beers she had consumed began to wear her down. At the edge of the stage, Dawson was waiting for her. He put her hands on her waist and lifted her up and then put her down gently next to him.

"You ready?" he asked with an odd expression on his face.

She nodded. "I think I might've overdone it."

"You can sleep it off tomorrow." Dawson helped her into her coat and walked behind her to the front door.

It had turned bitterly cold, and Marisa was shivering as she climbed into the passenger seat, grateful that Dawson had remotely turned on the truck and gotten the heat started. Then he got behind the wheel and leaned toward her to push the ignition button.

"You smell good," she said, and then let out a dainty burp. "Sorry."

He grinned. "I don't need to ask if you had a good time." Dawson put the truck in Reverse. He had stopped drinking hours ago after his second beer.

"No," she said, her eyes half-closed, as she used the seat controls to lean back her seat. "You probably don't."

"I'm taking you to your aunt and uncle's house."

"Shoot! That's right. I can't drive like this."

"No, you can't." And then asked, "What will your family think, me dropping you off?"

"I don't know. They are early to bed, early to rise kind of folks. I'll just tiptoe in and in the morning get up super early and tiptoe out to catch an Uber."

"Not so sure your plan is flawless but I wish you good luck. If you need me to pick you up and take you to the theater, the only payment I'll need is a smile."

"Dawson John! You are what *mi abuelita* would call a smooth talker."

"I'm also a truth talker and I want to see you as much as I can for as long as you'll let me."

She didn't seem to hear him. Instead she exclaimed, "Hey!" She reached over and tapped his arm with less than perfect precision. "My backside is getting toasty warm."

He nodded sagely, but there was a twinkle in his eye. "Heated seats."

"Oh," she said, closing her eyes. "I need to put these on my Christmas list."

The next morning, Dawson joined his family for their regular Saturday brunch. It was the one time during the week that their family came together. All of the siblings, plus wives and now a grandbaby.

"Now, Charity," Randall John said in his booming voice. "I've been getting all of this garbage on my phone, and I wish it would stop. It keeps on chiming, and beeping and buzzing and I don't want any of it, you hear?"

"Phone." Charity held out her hand.

She quickly searched his phone and then said, "Those are people reacting to my social media advertisements. It's a good thing, Dad."

Randall looked over to his wife. "Now what did she just say?"

"I'm sure I don't know," Mimi said. "What did you say, baby?"

"It's my advertising campaign for the Double J," Charity said but talked really slowly and a bit loudly.

"They can hear your words, Charity. They aren't deaf," Maddox said, bouncing his son in his arms. "Fast or slow, they aren't going to get it."

Charity rolled her eyes and made an annoyed noise in her throat. She had been handling the ranch's digital footprint, hiring a firm to revamp and maintain their website, using advertising dollars for social media, all the while tracking advertising reach and activity so she could adjust according to client interactions and interest.

"She's making deals, Dad," Jameson said. "But she doesn't use a handshake—she uses a computer."

"That's why our online sales have increased two hundred percent over the last year," Dawson added.

"Well," Randall said, "that's real nice, baby girl. Good work. Now, get it off of my phone."

Charity held out her hand again, took her father's phone, scrolled quickly and then handed it back to him. "I turned off notifications."

"Fine. Good." Randall slipped his phone back into his shirt pocket.

Dawson was just musing about how calm and peaceful this meal had been. There was usually some sort of drama or trauma being aired out at the family table. A few notifications from Facebook was pretty benign.

"What is this?" Mimi's eyes were glued to the screen of her phone. "Dawson. What have you done?" she said in a shocked whisper.

"So much for a quiet brunch," Charity muttered.

His mother looked up from her phone and repeated the question, her tone was very clipped.

"What now, Mimi?" Randall asked, followed by a frustrated sigh.

"What did you do?" Maddox asked him.

"You know exactly what he did," Jameson said as he continued to enjoy his breakfast. "Can you pass me those biscuits, Charity?"

Mimi reached for the newspaper still in the protective sleeve next to her husband's plate and opened it to the gossip column. She stared at it while a vein in her forehead began to bulge. "How could you do this, Dawson? Out in plain sight for everyone in Bronco to see!"

"Do what?" Dawson asked.

"You know exactly what you did, Dawson. And you know exactly why I wouldn't approve!" Mimi snapped.

"Now calm down, Mimi," Randall warned his wife. "You've got to watch that blood pressure."

"I wouldn't have high blood pressure if your son would do what he was born to do!"

"I'll take the baby," Maddox's wife, Adeline, said quietly, taking the child in her arms and leaving the dining room.

Mimi picked up the paper, slapped at it, and wrestling with it until she was able to flip it around. There on the gossip column page were several pictures of Marisa and him on the dance floor. The caption on the article was "Dawson John Gets Lucky."

"Oh, now, Mimi, that's nothing. He's just dancing like

boys do," Randall said, but Dawson knew that his mother would not be thrown off the scent.

"He's a man, not a boy," Mimi said with a biting tone, "and he should know better. You're toying with that young lady, and even though you don't often show it, I raised you better. She comes from a good family who values tradition…"

"But not good enough to carry the John name. I'm not toying with her, Mom. You're dead wrong on that point," Dawson said with an edge to his voice that he had never used with his mother before. "Marisa *is* from a good family. A top-notch family from my vantage point. And she sure is heck worthy of the John name or the Taylor name or the Abernathy name or any damn name she chooses. You're just too focused on appearances to see it!"

The table went quiet. Then Mimi stood up, dropped her napkin on her plate and, with her head held high, said, "I will not sit here and field insults from my own son." Mimi paused with her hands gripping the back of her chair, and Dawson's stomach twisted when he saw that his mother had unshed tears in her eyes. "There's a lot about the world you don't yet know about, Dawson. And clearly, my mistake was spoiling you." His mother walked out of the dining room stiffly.

Everyone looked at each other in confusion. Charity got up and said, "I'll go," following her mother to try and calm her down.

"Dawson," Randall said with a tone that brooked no argument, "you need to apologize to your mother. She brought you into this world. You might not agree with her, and that's your right, but you will damn well show her the respect that she is due."

"I will, Dad." Dawson said, "That…didn't go as I had planned."

Randall looked at him with disbelief. "Oh, it didn't? Looks to me like you wanted to push your mama's buttons, and I believe you succeeded."

Dawson had to admit to himself that his father was right. Yes, he did know that he would end up in the gossip column again eventually and then after the shock of it, a conversation would be had.

Wasn't that why, initially, he'd tried to go to out-of-the-way places with Marisa? To avoid all this? He sighed.

"Well, I am sorry," Dawson said to his father. The rest of his family quietly finished their food and quickly left the table to start their days. "I didn't mean to hurt Mom's feelings."

"Maybe not, but you did."

"I just want her to give Marisa a chance. That's all. One chance."

Randall rested his forearms on the table, fork and knife still in hand, and he pinned him with an intense gaze that made Dawson sit up straighter.

"Now you listen here, son. What your mama wants and what I want—there is no daylight between them. We want you to marry a girl who can handle ranch life because it's a tough life. We may not be the richest ranching family in town—yeah, I know it. Just don't let your mother ever hear me admit it. But we have a lot of land and a lot of responsibility."

Randall went back to pushing his brisket hash around his plate, then put his fork down and looked at his son. "The problem with you is that you've never struggled, you've never been without wealth and the influence that comes with it. But I promise you this, son, if you ever lost it, you'd do whatever you could to get it back. Your mother just wants the best for all you kids and to see that our grand-children and great grandchildren are provided for. And that none of you ever have to struggle to build a legacy the way we did, even if you still have to work hard. After all, there's nothing wrong with hard work."

"Understood, Dad," Dawson said.

"Listen, I can see that this isn't going to be the last we see of Marisa. I've got two good eyes and so does your mama. But for now, all you are going to do is apologize and thank your mother for doing her very best to take care of her family."

After his father left the room, Dawson sat at the dining table alone with his uneaten breakfast on his plate and no appetite for cold eggs and now-soggy toast. And he still sat, trying to process the scene that had just unfolded. In his younger years, he'd be off to the next adventure, his mother's feelings be damned. But now? He'd grown and he had changed. And it hurt him that he had hurt his mother so deeply.

Charity walked into the dining room, came around the table and hugged him.

"How's Mom?"

"Better. Resting." Charity said, "Don't be too hard on her, Dawson. She does want what's best for us, even if we disagree on how to get there."

"I know she thinks she knows what's best." After a moment, Dawson said to his sister, "I have real strong feelings for Marisa, Charity. Real strong."

"I know you do," Charity said. "So do I."

He didn't say it aloud, but he knew in his heart that Marisa was his future, and no matter what he needed to do to get his parents to accept her, he was going to do it.

Chapter Nine

Monday morning, Marisa was back at work with rehearsals. She had nursed a hangover most of Saturday and then had to explain herself when more pictures of Dawson and her looking very cuddly and enamored with each other appeared for a second day in a row in the *Bronco Bulletin*. She had known that going out with Dawson John would cause some ripples, but pictures in the newspaper with the caption "Outsider Waltzes Her Way into Dawson's Heart?" was much more exposure than she had wanted or anticipated.

"Good morning, Agnes," Marisa said, folding the Sunday paper and tucking it into the compartment on the piano seat.

Agnes handed her a cup of cocoa with three jumbo marshmallows. "So I gather you had a good time Friday night."

Like Agnes, everyone in Bronco had probably seen the paper. "Not enough to ruin the show." She sat down heavily and drank the hot chocolate down, ignoring the burn on her tongue, the roof of her mouth and down her throat.

"You didn't ruin the show," Agnes said. "In fact, if I know my Bronco the way I think I do, you're going to be filling even the cheap seats up there in the balcony. Everyone is going to want to know who this mysterious outsider is. It's not every day that a filly manages to lasso Dawson John's heart."

"Can we please stop speaking in metaphors? I'm not a filly and I haven't done anything to Dawson's heart."

"Okay. So you're in denial. Not a bad thing considering everything that is left to do before the show."

"Are you being helpful now, Agnes?"

"No," Agnes said, unfazed. "Probably not. I think you'd better sit down."

"I am sitting…"

"Then stay seated."

"Please don't say something like—"

"Your drummer is in the hospital."

"Are you serious?"

"As a heart attack."

"But I just saw him on Friday! Is he okay?"

"Heart attack," Agnes said. "Needs surgery."

Marisa had dropped her head into her hands, but then she looked up and said, "Agnes, that was a terrible turn of phrase in light of the fact that he actually *did* have a heart attack!"

"I know," the older woman agreed. "I caught that right after I said it. At my age, sometimes it comes out right and sometimes it doesn't."

Dawson had stayed in contact with Marisa via text, but he had backed away after three days of gossip column photos. Monday the caption said, "More than Just Friends?" He had apologized to his mother. Meant it sincerely, but the daily pictures in the newspaper overshadowed everything else, including the apology. His mom was not moving from her position that he needed to find a wife from a landholding cattle family and if she was a debutante how could that hurt? But he was rock solid on his position too; these feelings he had for Marisa had only grown with time. This was not a phase; this was not a fling. This was something much deeper than he'd ever felt before.

After a couple of days, Dawson realized that all he

wanted was to spend as much time as possible with Marisa. Surely his mother would eventually recover from the reality of his relationship with Marisa, but he knew that if he lost his chance with the lovely director, he believed that *recovery* wouldn't be possible.

Monday evening, after all of the performers had gone home for the night, Agnes let him into the locked theater before she switched off the lights and headed home.

"Don't leave any lights on, Dawson. You don't pay the light bill around here."

"Yes, ma'am."

He walked through the same door that he had walked through the first day he had met Marisa. It was only a couple of weeks ago but it felt to him like a lifetime. The seating area was dark while the only real light was coming from the stage where Marisa was sitting cross-legged, sifting through sheet music.

"Agnes let me in," he called out, not really knowing how to get her attention without scaring the wits out of her.

Marisa did start, but once she recognized his voice, she nodded her head and waved him over to the stage. He climbed up the steps and walked over to her.

She stood up, met him halfway and hugged him. Until that very moment, he had no idea how much he needed that hug.

"Are you okay?" she asked.

He leaned back to look down at her angelic face. "Are you?"

She nodded. "I think so. Agnes thinks free publicity is good publicity. The theater website has had a lot of traffic and ticket sales are up, so..." She shrugged. "Maybe she's right."

Dawson reached for the long, thick braid of her hair,

so shiny and black and sexy on her. "That's one way to look at it."

"What's another way?" she asked, and he saw the sincere concern in her eyes.

"It's been a little rough around the Double J."

"I was afraid of that. Charity came in this morning looking like she hadn't gotten any sleep, and she left early."

"She takes it hard when our family gets to fighting."

"Fighting…about me?"

"Yes and no."

"Am I solving a riddle?" she asked him, and he could tell that Marisa had been feeling added pressure from the attention.

"It's not about you. It's about me," he told her honestly. "I've never fallen in line. I've always thought I'm the third son, why do I have to stay on any path other than the one I forge for myself? They have certain expectations for their children and I haven't been inclined to meet those expectations."

"They don't approve of me."

"It's complicated."

A flash of raw hurt swept across her face and she turned away from him. "Why don't you just tell them that I'm leaving at the end of November. I'm not a threat."

Dawson walked around to face her, took her hands in his and waited for her to look up in to his face.

"Hey," he said. "It hasn't been long since we first met but we have been honest with each other, haven't we?"

She nodded. "I have."

"And so have I," he said. "You mean something to me, Marisa. You *mean* something to *me*."

When she looked up at him, he saw tears streaming down her face; he wiped them away and for the second time in one week, kicked himself because he'd made one of the two most important women in his life cry.

"You mean something to me too, Dawson." Marisa stole her hands away to wipe the rest of the tears from her face. "I don't know what that something is, but it's there."

"Then don't build a wall up between us," he said, and then next words represented sentiments he had never felt before Marisa. "I need you."

Her eyes widened with both surprise and fear and it took her much longer than he would have liked to respond. When she did, she said, "I—feel," another pause, "that I may need you in my life right now."

Dawson furrowed his brow. "Not exactly the level of enthusiasm I was hoping for but I suppose it's a start."

Marisa could see that Dawson wanted to move on from the gossip column and the turmoil it had created in both of their lives, so she introduced a neutral topic that involved the pageant. Dawson, from the very beginning, had been a reliable sounding board for all things pageant.

"Did you hear about my drummer?"

"I did."

Marisa bent down to collect the sheet music she had strewn across the stage floor. "He has surgery tomorrow."

"Have you found a replacement?"

"Thankfully, yes," she said. "I'd hoped to get my drummer from Tenacity, but he's out of town until a day before our show."

"Figures."

"But one of my old bandmates…" She stopped and looked at him. "Do you even know that I was in a band?"

He nodded. "I follow you on all the social media platforms, we are Facebook friends and I subscribed to your

YouTube channel. Row House Four was the name of your college band."

"Well, thank you. That wasn't stalkerish at all." She laughed and he felt gratified. There it was, that warm, tingling feeling that he got whenever he was with Marisa. It was a feeling he was beginning to wonder if he could manage to live without.

"My life took a different path but the band still gigs in Boston. My drummer, Shira Weiss, will be flying out to fill in at the show," she said. "I am so thankful to have such a good friend who also plays a mean tumbak."

"Definition needed."

She laughed again. "It's a hand drum that is played seated with the base between the thighs. It's one of the oldest instruments from India and it really adds a cool vibe to the songs."

He shook his head, fascinated with Marisa's appreciation for other cultures and finding ways to weave their dancing, their instruments into American classics.

After she put the sheet music away in a file cabinet just beyond the curtain, Marisa turned around and saw that Dawson was standing in the middle of the stage with a very peculiar look on his ridiculously handsome face.

"What's going on?"

"Come here," he said.

She walked over to him, curiously. "What do you have in your pocket? More marshmallows?"

"No." He patted the pocket in his shirt. "I keep those right here."

"You don't!" She laughed. "Do you?"

Dawson pulled a small bag of marshmallows out of his shirt pocket and Marisa felt seen and appreciated and yes, loved. Such a simple gesture spoke more to her heart in a way that a thousand red roses and thousands of words could ever say.

"You're not all the way here yet," Dawson said, his feet slightly apart, his hands clasped in front of his body, waiting for her arrival.

"Well," she said, slowly walking on purpose now. "It's after hours, we are the only souls in this old, creaky building, the wind is howling outside and you are luring me—"

"Luring is a very strong word."

"*Luring* me over to you." She repeated the word with more conviction. "And you have something for me in your pocket. What do you have Dawson? Should I be worried?"

"You have taken this to a really dark place," he said with a smile. "Maybe I'm the one who sould be worried about you?"

"No. Ask anyone. I'm super sweet and totally harmless."

"Jury is still out on both counts."

She finally reached him and that was when he pulled a sprig of mistletoe out of his pocket.

Marisa put her hands up to her mouth, her eyes shining with surprise and delight. "Mistletoe, Dawson?"

"Mistletoe, Marisa." Then he said, "Do you believe in the magic of mistletoe?"

She put her hands on her lovely hips. "That's my line! You're stealing my lines, Dawson."

"And I'm trying to steal a kiss."

And then you'll try to steal my heart.

Dawson held the sprig over her head and then, giving her ample time to stop what was coming, he touched his lips to hers and that spark of energy sizzled between them. It was a quick, soft kiss, but for her, she could feel the vibration of his heart of gold when he touched his lips to hers.

Marisa still had her eyes shut and he took it as a direct

invitation to kiss her again. Stuffing the mistletoe into his pocket, Dawson drew her into his arms, leaned down and kissed her how she had always imagined he would—deeply, passionately, and full of promise of good days yet to come. Marisa slowly opened her eyes and looked into his.

"Hmm," she murmured. "I wondered what that would be like."

"And?"

"Where's that mistletoe?" she asked in a languid, sexy voice she'd never used before.

"Right here." He pulled it out of his pocket.

Marisa took the sprig, grabbed his hand with her free one, and then led him over to the steps. She positioned him three steps down and facing her. Then, with a saucy, sassy expression on her face, she held the mistletoe over his head. Because he was several steps down, they stood eye to eye, lips to lips.

She kissed him as he had kissed her—with heat and passion—while they shared breath.

"You are full of surprises, Dawson John." Marisa touched the tips of her fingers to her lips.

He pulled her braid over her shoulder. "I can say the same about you."

Arm in arm, they walked down the steps together and Marisa picked up her backpack but Dawson lifted it off her shoulder and hooked it onto his, as he always did.

"Are you hungry?" he asked her.

"Famished," she admitted. "I love rehearsals, but they can be a real grind."

"Pizza?"

"Greasy?"

"No other way to eat it."

She stopped walking, so he stopped. "Are we sure we

want to venture out into public again? One night at Wild Willa's Saloon and we made the gossip column three days in a row. And Charity was really upset. It hurt me to see *her* hurt so much. It must have been a bad scene at your house."

"I know. It was. And I'm sorry that Charity got caught up in it," Dawson said with an edge in his tone. "But I'm just living my life here. That's it. I like you and I want to buy you a slice of pizza. Do you want to eat pizza with me?"

She nodded.

"Then let's just do it, Marisa. Life's too damn short."

"Made shorter by eating cheesy, greasy pizza."

"I'm serious, Marisa."

"I know you are."

He held out his hand for her. "So?"

She took a moment, then slipped her hand into his. "So, okay."

He couldn't help but smile. "Well, okay then."

Marisa had wolfed down three slices of pizza, and then she felt satisfied.

"Rate the pizza," Dawson said.

"Ten out of ten, for sure."

Dawson wasn't done so she felt content to sip her soda and enjoy looking at all of his handsomeness.

"I have a confession to make," she said, and heard shyness in her voice.

"Oh yeah?"

"I've spent more time than I'd like to admit surfing through your social media content."

He stopped chewing to smile a closed-mouth smile.

"Stop it!" She felt her cheeks flush.

He swallowed down his last piece of pizza with a long swig of soda. "So, did you like what you saw?"

"Honestly, it made me wonder if you own enough shirts. You were bare chested climbing mountains, bare chested BASE jumping off a bridge—illegal by the way—shirtless riding a horse, white water rafting, biking, hiking, zip lining, working out in the gym and paragliding. The only time you had a shirt on was for skydiving."

"They made me keep my shirt on."

"It's hard for me to believe that those abs are real," she said. "I mean who has abs like that?"

"Me."

"You're all muscled and tan and your abs are so defined that it looks like someone painted them on right before the pictures were taken."

"All natural, baby," he said, and wiggled his eyebrows up and down. "Want to cop a feel?"

"You quit it, Dawson!" She leaned forward and whispered harshly, "No more pictures in the paper!"

"Oh come on…be a sport." He laughed. "How about this caption—'Marisa Sanchez grabs more than a slice of pizza'?"

It was oddly easy with Dawson—they laughed, they challenged each other and they had been a shoulder for the other to lean on. And, as a total bonus, he was smoking hot and kissed like nothing she had ever experienced before. She would be reliving and replaying those mistletoe kisses for many years to come.

"Now, you are an adrenaline junkie," she said. "Charity was right about that. I can't believe how many places you have traveled just to put yourself in harm's way!"

"You could join me."

"Dawson, really? Do I look like an extreme sports enthusiast?"

He wiped his mouth with a napkin, then balled it up and

dropped it onto his plate. "How do I know if I don't ask? You've got a wild side, I can sense it."

"Wishful thinking, more like it."

He smiled and winked at her again, leaning back in his seat, his body language open and confident. "How do you land on zip lining?"

She wrinkled her brow and her nose in thought. "I land on the side of 'no, not happening.' I will not let some stranger strap me into a safety harness when I have not personally investigated the safety and maintenance of that piece of equipment, and put my life in the hands of some dude—"

"Could be a chick. Sexist."

"Who is most likely high on skunk weed," she said, "while he pushes me off of a perfectly good platform and sends me hurling through the atmosphere on a tiny rope—"

"It's a very strong cable."

"Through trees! And what? I hope I make it to the other platform without smacking my head on a wayward tree limb or crash into the platform because this contraption they have put me on doesn't have brakes!"

Dawson listened to her, grinning from ear to ear. "Are you finished?"

She crossed her arms over her chest. "For now, yes."

"So, I'll put you down as a 'no' for zip lining?"

She nodded once. "Emphatic no. Hard pass."

"Where do you land on white water rafting?"

The next couple of days after their first kiss, Marisa was grateful for her work so she could focus her attention on something other than missing Dawson. He had told her after he took her out for pizza that he would be helping Bronco set up for the Mistletoe Rodeo that always got started right after the Mistletoe Pageant. She hadn't expected to miss him as much as she did, and at weak moments she felt like crying. Of course, she was completely stressed out and exhausted—perhaps missing Dawson was that straw that broke the camel's back.

"Marisa!"

Marisa turned toward the door to the theater and saw her dear friend Shira Weiss running down the stairs toward her. Shira had shoulder length black hair with purple braids on either side of her head making her look like she was sporting a modified mohawk. Her eyebrows were black and they framed her light green and gold catlike eyes in the loveliest of ways. She had always been a slender, fit young woman who was bursting with positive energy and excitement for life in general.

Shira barreled over to her and threw her arms around her and rocked back and forth.

"Thank you so much for coming, Shira!"

"You bet," her friend said, her hands on her hips, surveying the environment. "This place is incredible."

"I think so too," Marisa agreed. "It can be drafty at times, but I really like it."

Marisa hugged Shira again; she felt so grateful that she would come all the way to Montana to help her pull off this job.

"You'll be staying at my aunt and uncle's house with me."

"Cool," Shira said.

"That way you won't feel so homesick for Thanksgiving."

Shira smiled at her, adjusting the Star of David necklace that she rarely took off.

"As long as I make it back in time for Hanukah, we're good."

Marisa gave Shira all of the music that she had provided to the Bronco-based band. The drummer knew many of these arrangements, so it wouldn't take her long to get up to speed for the show.

Chapter Ten

Marisa was working furiously to pull all of the loose strings together as the town of Bronco anticipated the Mistletoe Pageant, which then led into the Mistletoe Rodeo. And even though she'd made changes based on the focus group and Dawson's insight, Marisa still felt out of her depth with this show. It was still a mystery who had ultimately recommended her for the job—not to mention hired her for this milestone event that was so steeped in Bronco tradition. But she was determined not to let anyone down—including herself.

"Hold up!" Marisa waved her hands at the dancers while she took the stairs up to the stage. "That's not the correct sequence for this song. Here, let me show you." Marisa nodded to Charity who had taken it upon herself to record the band's version of each song in the show so they could practice dancing and singing without needing the band at the theater. There would be rehearsals with the band coming up; for now, Marisa needed fewer people, not more, in the room.

Marisa worked with the dancers for a few minutes, demonstrating the steps then running the sequence a couple of times. Then she headed back down the steps so she could watch the dancers from the vantage of the audience.

"Yes!" Marisa clapped out the beat with her hands. "Yes! That's it! Now you're on track!"

Marisa gave Charity two thumbs-up. How would she have managed without her? So talented, so willing to pitch in. As much as her feelings had grown for Dawson, she loved Charity apart from him. And she hoped that no matter what, Charity and she would continue a friendship beyond this one show.

She turned away from the stage when her phone rang and she saw Dawson's name on the screen. "Hi!" she said as she walked to a more private spot. "I was just thinking about you."

"I was just thinking about you."

"How are the rodeo preps going?"

"Almost done."

"Wow! Already?"

"What can I say? Manpower, baby."

Marisa laughed, her mood buoyed by Dawson's phone call. Ever since he started helping with the rodeo, he didn't have as much time to stop by the theater as before. So, she was glad that he was wrapping up preparations.

"I'd like to see you tomorrow," he said, sending her heart racing. "What's your schedule look like?"

"Rehearsals in the morning, but I'm letting everyone off in the afternoon. Everyone is slaphappy. They need a break."

"I'm in luck, then."

"What did you have in mind?" Marisa began to imagine an intimate lunch for two, or sitting together in a movie theater sharing a big tub of popcorn, or even sitting close on a bench in the park across from city hall drinking hot chocolate and watching city employees set up the holiday decorations.

"Hiking."

"Hiking?" she asked as if he had suggested robbing a bank or stealing a car. "Are you crazy? Why do you think I would want to brave the cold, which will only get colder as we climb?" She shuddered. "Climb, what a horrible word."

"Have you ever gone hiking?" he asked. "It can be exhilarating. Out in the elements, back to nature, seeing wildlife up close and personal…"

"You are making a great case for why I don't like to hike. But for your information, yes, I've hiked with my brothers on Tenacity Trail."

"That's a really nice beginner trail."

"You've hiked it?"

"Of course," he said. "I've been to Tenacity too. I like your hometown."

"Well, if that trail is for beginners, I'm an infant. And I'm an infant that doesn't appreciate activities that involve no restaurants, or climate control, and offer a chance that I could fall on icy rocks and break my tailbone or be eaten alive by a hungry bear.

"In conclusion, why would I want to go hiking with you?" she asked him.

"Because I'll be there."

Marisa frowned and then after a couple of heartbeats, she said, "In that case, I'll go. But I get to pick our next adventure. Deal?"

"Deal."

The next day, Dawson picked Marisa up at the theater, and he drove them to an intermediate trail just outside of Bronco. He had chosen this trail because after seeing Marisa dance for hours without much effort, he believed that she had more stamina than she gave herself credit for.

"I'm glad to see you," he told her.

"I'm glad to see you!" Marisa agreed.

He had missed this woman more than he had ever missed anyone in his life. It had only been a couple of days that they hadn't seen each other in person but they had video chatted, talked on the phone and texted. It made him wonder if he was being an absolute fool to think that he could ever give her up. No, his parents were not on board and had told him without one shred of ambiguity that Marisa Sanchez was not John material. And that comment from his mother at brunch had so infuriated him that he'd spent the night on a friend's couch until he cooled off.

"Penny for your thoughts."

He could feel Marisa's gaze on his face, and it occurred to him that she could read him now in the same way he could read her. It had happened so quickly, this knowing each other, but wasn't that strong evidence to support their uncanny connection? Even if his parents never ceded this point, Dawson didn't care.

He reached over, squeezed her hand. "I was just thinking that I missed you."

Marisa made a sound of relief. "Okay, good. At least I wasn't the only one."

"You missed me?"

She nodded. "More than I should have, I think."

"How much is too much?"

"I don't know."

Neither did he and that was a fact. Now was the time to hike and have fun, and he certainly hoped to offer her his warm body as her own personal heater and he had every intention of kissing her when they reached the peak. Dawson had never wanted to create memories with any woman before. Most of his social media had been focused on extreme sports; in fact, his exes often complained that because he refused to post pictures of them that he wasn't serious about them. Maybe they were right; he'd already posted Marisa on his social media several times. If the *Bronco*

Bulletin was going to keep putting them in the gossip column, why shouldn't he post?

"That's a long way up." Marisa put her hand on her forehead so she could block the light and gaze at the peak.

"It's not as bad as you think…"

She waved her hands at his body. "Says Adonis!"

Dawson smiled at her with a wink at being compared to a Greek god.

"Okay," she said with a grumpy tone of voice, "stop basking and let's go so I can make an immediate U-turn at the top and get back into this nice warm truck."

Dawson just grinned at her. He strapped on a backpack with supplies and led the way.

"I've never been allergic to bee stings, but just in case my body decides to go rogue on me, do you have an EpiPen?"

"Got it."

"There isn't a cloud in the sky, but I get sick whenever I get rained on…and if I get sick, there won't be any show…"

"I have ponchos."

"I didn't eat lunch. You picked me up right after rehearsals, and I didn't have a chance to even eat a granola bar. I tend to be hypoglycemic—I could get lightheaded and dizzy and then fall off of the side of the cliff…"

"I packed a picnic for us."

Dawson had never been on a hike with a person who complained that much but because it was Marisa and he thought she was adorable, he wasn't feeling irritated by it yet. Normally if someone was ruining his good time, he didn't wait—he dumped them and went on with his life. But Marisa was in a special category—a totally new category—so she was getting a lot of latitude from him.

"You are very prepared," Marisa grumbled.

He laughed and turned back to her, put her round face in his hands and kissed her. "You sound disappointed."

"Mmm, I feel less cranky now," she said. "Kiss me again!"

Five more kisses later, Marisa made it all the way to the halfway point before she couldn't continue. Her face was flushed from the cold air, but also from the exertion of hiking up an incline.

They sat down on one of the benches placed along the trail specifically for this reason. He handed her a bottle of water and a high energy, low sugar protein bar.

"How is it?" he asked.

"Tastes like Elmer's glue."

"I'm not even going to ask how you know that."

She chewed some more, washed down the last of the bar with water, put the cap back on, and then said, "I teach Bible school over the summer. I know what glue tastes like, trust me."

He smiled at her, put his arm around her, pulled her close and kissed the top of her head, which had been fortified with a very thick crocheted toboggan beanie.

"I think you're pretty amazing, Marisa."

When he gave her an unexpected compliment, Marisa actually turned shy for a split second, and her cheeks turned a deeper shade of pink. That blush on her cheeks was his reward. He found himself staring at her face, making a mental map of her petite nose, her dark eyelashes, tigress eyes and those full lips that made kissing her his favorite new pastime.

"Thank you, Dawson," she said quietly. "I think you're pretty amazing yourself."

"Then it's mutual."

She nodded. "Very much so."

He stood up, put the backpack on, then held out his hand for her. She took it and groaned when she stood up and had to straighten her back.

"I'm going to pay for this tomorrow, aren't I?"

"Maybe even tonight," he said easily. "Ready?"

While fielding many complaints about a slippery rock, a narrow trail, an industrious woodpecker that would surely attack her, and bears that would come out of hibernation just to eat her as a snack, Dawson managed to push Marisa to make it to the peak.

His companion stood near the edge of the rocky top of the mountain and looked back at the trail she had hiked to reach the peak. Her jacket was tied at her waist, and she drank down an entire bottle of water in seconds. Hands on her hips, her lovely chest rising and falling quickly, Marisa wiped the sweat from her brow.

"I can't believe you got me up here, Dawson."

He walked to stand beside her. "You got yourself up here, Marisa."

"You were so patient with me, encouraging, you knew when to let me have a break and when I needed to push through so I wouldn't lose momentum. You are an amazing coach. How did you learn to do that?"

"I don't know." He twisted the cap off of his water bottle. "I've never done it before."

Marisa looked over at him. "Never?"

"If someone doesn't want to go hiking, I leave them behind. If someone gets tired. I leave them behind."

"You never left me behind."

"No." He studied his companion's face—a face he had grown to love. "I didn't."

He was quiet for a moment and then he added, "I guess I should take a hard look at what makes you so different from just about anyone else on the planet."

Marisa stood at the peak and felt a sense of accomplishment that she hadn't expected. Dawson was right, she did feel a hiker's high and it lasted for a while. Then, the sweat on her skin began to make her feel chilled all over her body and she began to shiver. She untied her jacket from around her waist and put it on.

"Cold?" Dawson asked after he picked up the remnants of their picnic.

She nodded, her teeth chattering.

"Come here," he said. "Let me warm you up."

Dawson opened his jacket while she scooted closer to him. With his arm around her, Marisa felt cared for by this man who had turned her life upside down and every which way. It wasn't like her at all to play hooky to follow a cowboy, who also happened to be an adrenaline junkie, up to the top of a mountain! But this moment, cuddling with Dawson in a room with the best view nature could provide, was all the reward she needed for the challenging climb she had just completed.

"Better?" he asked.

She nodded, tilted her head back and looked into his eyes, which were filled with so much acceptance and dare she think...love? He cupped her face with his hands and kissed her sweetly. She leaned in, put her hand behind his head to offer him more and he took it. He deepened the kiss while his large hand slid into her jacket and cupped her breast. Every place on her body felt like it was on fire, her chill long forgotten, while warmth and tingling rushed from her toes, to her throat, to her fingers and her lips. It had been so long since she had let any man touch her like this; it had been such a long time since she had been kissed. But never in her life had she felt so desired, cherished, needed by any man. In both word and deed, Dawson was telling her that he cared.

"I think I'm warm enough now," she said, ending the lovers' embrace.

He gave her one final kiss on the lips. "I'm glad I could help. Ready to do the easiest part of this hike?"

"Yes, sir, I most certainly am!"

When they arrived back in Bronco, they were stopped by a police unit blocking the road including trucks for the local TV station KBTV.

"I wonder what's happening here," Marisa said, sitting forward in her seat.

"I don't know," Dawson said, "but at least they aren't trying to photograph us again."

Marisa looked at her phone to see if there were any real-time reports and her mood deflated. "Oh, no! This can't be."

"What?"

She showed him a link to the *Bronco Bulletin*'s home page. "Someone left a baby in a basket in the church vestibule!" This news hit Marisa hard. She had wanted to be a mother for so long but, so far, she hadn't met the father of her children. On the back end of her twenties, she was conscious that fertility declined significantly by thirty-five and she had truly begun to prepare herself to accept the idea that she might not have children. For someone to have a precious baby, a blessed gift from God above, and chose to leave it at a church, in the middle of winter, was very difficult for her to understand and even more challenging for her to forgive.

"Who would do such a thing?" she asked, upset.

"Someone desperate, I reckon."

She nodded but didn't speak for fear that she might start to cry.

He looked over at her, must have seen her pain, and reached for her hand. He took it in his and squeezed it to give her comfort.

"Do they say anything else?" he asked her.

"No. Nothing."

Once Dawson parked his truck in the theater parking lot, they both joined the gathering crowd. "I thought someone had left a doll," a church employee was saying when they got close enough to hear the ongoing press conference that had been set up in front of the church. "But then I realized it was a real baby! That's when I called the authorities and they're on the job now, so I feel like I've played my part in God's plan for this innocent child."

A reporter shouted a question. "Any idea who the mother might be?"

"No. No. I surely don't. I'll cooperate with the authorities, of course," the church worker said.

Another reporter asked, "What happens to the baby now?"

This time one of Bronco's police took the question. Marisa recognized Officer Lopez as he moved behind the mic and said, "The baby will be put in the care of social services until a suitable foster home can be located. And that's it for now, folks. We have work to do."

As the crowd dispersed, Marisa felt heartbroken for that little baby. "Marisa?" Dawson was steadfast by her side. "What's wrong?"

"I have always wanted to be a mom just like my mother. It's hard to believe that someone could be gifted with a child and then abandon it."

"The baby is in good hands now," he said. "This town comes together and helps each other out in a crisis or a pinch."

She hoped that was true. Her arms crossed over her chest, and her mind still with the baby, Marisa walked beside Dawson back to the theater.

"Are you going to be okay?" he asked her when they reached their destination.

"Yes." She nodded. "Of course. I just have a tender heart for children."

He reached for her braid and pulled it over her shoulder. This was something that Dawson just liked to do and she liked it. It made her feel connected to him.

"Well, get some rest tonight. Your big show is only two days away."

"Two days!" She gave a shake of her head. "So much to do! I've got to get my head back in the game. But—" she smiled up at him "—thank you for today. You got me to do something that I didn't really think that I could do." She raised her arms up like Rocky after a prizefight. "I conquered the intermediate trail!"

"Yes, you did. Can I talk you in to the advanced trail after all of this holiday craziness settles down?"

This was the first time Dawson had ever spoken of a future between them after the show and after she had returned to Tenacity. In her mind, when she looked into the future, she still couldn't see Dawson there with her, living the quiet life of a family man. That was what she had dreamed of since she was a little girl helping her mother in the kitchen. It had been an old-fashioned model that wasn't really on-brand for her as the progressive game changer. But Marisa accepted that she was a whole, complicated person and she had a right to her own dreams.

"It's hard for me to even imagine life after this show!"

"I'm going to be in the front row supporting Charity and you both."

Instinctively, and not looking around to see if paparazzi were hiding in the bushes, Marisa hugged Dawson.

"Thank you, Dawson," she said. "You've helped me so much from beginning to end."

"All I did was help you change up your playlist, that's all."

"No," she told him. "You did much more than that."

Dawson had to leave to meet his brothers at the rodeo site while she headed back into the theater to wrap her mind around the next steps.

"Hi, sweetie." Agnes walked into the lounge that, at times, became her office.

"Hi, Agnes."

"We're in the home stretch."

"Yes, we are."

"How are you holding up?" Agnes said, putting on a fresh pot of coffee.

"Surprisingly well, really. I thought I would be a total mess. Maybe that will happen right after the curtain closes."

Agnes joined her at the table. "Did you hear about the baby in the church? Poor thing. I wish there was something we could do."

Marisa bit her lip. "I had an idea, but I'm not sure we would be allowed to do this. But…it might just help get more word out about the little one."

Agnes looked at her. "What idea?"

"Well," Marisa said, closing the lid of her computer. "What if we could shine a spotlight on his case by having him star as our baby in the manger? Of course we'd talk to all the proper channels for permission, and we'd make sure his guardian is there every step of the way. But really, you never know. Someone in the audience might just have some information."

"Do you know what, Marisa? I think that's an incredible idea!"

"Let's find out who we need to get approval!" Marisa said, excited. "We're going to do our best to help this little one find his family for Christmas gift!"

Chapter Eleven

The day of the Mistletoe Pageant, Marisa donned a dress that flattered her figure while the deep red displayed her Christmas cheer. She added the touch of wreath earrings and a matching wreath broach. She loved all of the holidays in her show, but her family celebrated Christmas in accordance with their faith, and Three Kings Day, in accordance with her Hispanic heritage.

"How's the house?" Agnes came up behind her while she was peeking out of the curtain.

"It's filling up, Agnes."

Marisa stepped back from the curtain and pressed her fingers into the corners of her eyes to stop tears of anxiety, stress, happiness and relief all balled up together.

"Oh, come here, baby doll." Agnes put her arms around her and hugged her. "You've done an amazing job, Marisa. I would tell you if you didn't."

"I know you would." Marisa laughed. And laughter was just what she needed.

The back of the stage was bustling and buzzing with excitement and nerves; Marisa pushed away her own feelings to focus on making sure every performer had a personal moment with her to discuss any last minute questions or concerns. Focusing on others had served her well in the past.

"All of the costumes are on point!" a singer called out to her. "Your mom is a genius!"

Marisa walked around a corner and found Sam Scott and Shira talking. By their body language, this wasn't the first time they had spoken alone. And the way Sam was smiling down at her friend and the way her friend was smiling up at the carpenter, Marisa was certain that some sparks would be flying while Shira was still in town.

"You did great!" Shira hugged her. "This is one of your best shows. I can feel it!"

"Are the sets up to your standards?" Sam asked her.

"You are a miracle worker, Sam. I came here with some props from Tenacity, but I'm bringing back art pieces you have created. Tenacity will be enjoying these beautiful creations for years to come."

Knowing that she could use the props for her regular gig as director and producer of the Tenacity holiday show, she had used money from her Tenacity budget to have Sam build the new props.

"I'm glad you're pleased."

"The manger? It is a masterpiece, Sam."

Marisa walked away, but she was still in earshot when her sassy friend said to Sam, "I love a man who is good with his hands."

Marisa kept right on walking, but said to herself with a smile, "Flirt!"

On her last round, she ran into a woman carrying a large arrangement of flowers. It was so large that Marisa couldn't see the entire top half of the woman's body—only legs down.

"Oh, Ms. Sanchez, I found you. These are for you. Where should I put them?"

"Is there a card?"

The bouquet was made of flowers that were a nod to her Mexican heritage while incorporating her favorite colors of yellow and purple. She plucked a daisy from the bouquet and tucked it behind her ear.

"Right here," the woman said.

"Thank you." She took the envelope. "Can you manage to get this to the lounge?"

"Yes, I can."

She opened the envelope and read the note. "Break a leg, Marisa. You've got this! Dawson."

She held the note to her chest and then tucked it into a side pocket of her dress. At that moment, Charity came full-tilt around a corner and barely had time to stop before running smack dab into her.

"Marisa!" Charity was bubbling over with performance day excitement. "Thank you so much for this opportunity! I love you. Is that okay for me to say? I love you. I hope we're friends forever."

Marisa hugged Charity and said, "We will be friends. Forever. Now go out there tonight and show this town just what a triple threat Charity John is!"

"I will!"

And then, just like a snap of the fingers, all of her worry, all of her work, all of her putting out fires, all of her questions and doubts and revising of plans disappeared. It was time to start the show.

Marisa walked out to the stage and stood in front of the closed curtain. The lights were lowered and a hush fell over the crowd. Right in the front row, Dawson was sitting with his parents, his siblings and their wives. She didn't look at him directly, but the daisy she wore tucked back behind her ear was a message just for him.

When the applause subsided, she continued. "Tonight

we have a very special guest, Baby J, playing the role of baby Jesus in the manger. Please be very quiet when he is onstage and only clap after he has been taken backstage. Thank you so much, Bronco! Please enjoy the show!"

Dawson sat beside his mother while they waited for the show to begin. They still weren't on the best of terms over the gossip column fiasco, but there was something upon which they always agreed—their love and support for Charity. As long as they stuck to the topic of Charity, things ran pretty smoothly between them.

When Marisa walked out onto the stage he immediately noticed behind her ear she wore a daisy from her bouquet, and he knew that she had not only done this as a thank you to him but it was a way to keep him close to her. Marisa looked spectacular in that red dress, but she was always pretty to him with her round face, her dark eyes, sexy curves and a smile that drew his attention time and again to her full, kiss-worthy lips that he taken to dreaming about.

He felt his mother's body tense next to him when Marisa appeared onstage, but to her credit, she pursed her lips and stifled even the tiniest of throat sounds. After Marisa took her seat behind the piano and the rest of the house lights dimmed, the band began to play and the curtain slowly opened. There on the stage was a vision the likes of which he had never seen: Charity standing alone with a spotlight on her. She was dressed in a modernized Mrs. Claus costume. Once Charity began to sing "White Christmas" acapella, a collective gasp could be heard from the audience. When he heard it, he closed his hand into a fist, hit his leg with it and thought to himself, *You did it, Marisa!* Right out of the gate, Marisa hit them with a beloved song that he'd told her was the most requested song at the local radio station.

Dawson had never felt as proud of anyone as he did of Marisa and Charity. They'd created a Mistletoe Pageant for the record books. Everything Marisa had done to marry her vision of bringing new musical styles and arrangements, with Bronco's usual pageant was masterful. And, every time Charity stepped out onto stage or sang a song or danced with the other performers, Mimi was clutching the arms of her chair so tightly that her knuckles went white.

Marisa had the audience in the palm of her hand. She played the piano, watched every move of the actors and dancers onstage and communicated with the live band. He could barely take his eyes off her.

When it came time for the traditional Nativity scene and Baby J was in the manger, surrounded by the three kings, Mary and Joseph, the audience was silent and respectful and Dawson believed that this would be the most talked about part of the most talked about show in the history of Bronco.

"I can't believe it's almost over," Mimi said to no one in particular.

Marisa played "Have Yourself a Merry Little Christmas" with her own arrangement while the cast made one last costume and set change. When Marisa finished the song, the audience clapped for her loudly and Dawson even heard some cheers. If this was a preview of what was to come after the last song, the cast would have to perform several encores.

The curtain opened and the entire cast was on the stage with Charity standing by herself in front of the others.

When Mimi made a sound in her throat, Dawson looked over at his mom, a woman whom he had never seen allow her social mask to slip in the slightest, and saw unshed tears in her eyes. He was at odds with both of his parents for the majority of his teenage and adult years and he supposed it always would be this way, but Mimi was still his mother. While the cast sang "We Wish You a Merry Christmas" with a classic arrangement, Dawson reached over to take his mother's hand. She held his hand tightly and even put her left hand on top of his.

"She's an angel, Dawson," she said in a wavering voice. "Do you see her?"

"I see her, Mom. I see her."

Mimi reached for her husband's hand and when Dawson leaned forward just a bit, he could see that his father was also stunned by his daughter. Charity was the youngest and the only daughter—it had been difficult for any of them, including him, to see her as a grown woman. After tonight, they were all going to have to rethink their relationship with Charity. Marisa saw in Charity what none of them really had before, and she had done her best to build up those raw gifts.

What Marisa had done for Charity only made him love her more. And it made him wonder—after everything Marisa had done for their daughter, would Randall and Mimi be open to the idea of her as a daughter-in-law?

Marisa sat at her piano and watched the final performance of the Bronco, Montana's, Mistletoe Pageant holiday show. She had deliberately omitted the piano from the last song so she could enjoy the performance. The night had been a triumph; it had and she knew it. Everything that she had wanted to accomplish—produce a show that would make Bronco feel at home in the theater, shine a light on Baby J, weave other cultural celebrations throughout while still maintaining the traditions that the town cherished—had been achieved, all with the hard work and support and dedication and talent that she had found in Bronco. As the last note of the last song was being sung, Marisa met Dawson's gaze and mouthed *thank you* to him. Dawson had saved this show for her, and if he hadn't cared about her and if he hadn't cared so much about Charity, this night would have surely turned out to be a disaster and might've just been a nuclear bomb on her career. She could easily imagine TikTok videos of her going viral, but this time for all the wrong reasons. Social media was, after all, a fickle lover.

When the curtain closed, Marisa was on her feet, clapping as hard as her hands would allow. She took the stairs and was there to continue clapping when the curtain reopened and the cast took another bow.

Marisa took a microphone, waited for the thunderous applause to die down and then she said, "Thank you, Bronco, for going on this incredible journey with me. I feel blessed and honored and all of the credit must go to the wonderful people standing behind me. Most of you know that I grew up not too far from here, in Tenacity. In my house, at Christmastime, there is a song that I sang with my family."

She turned her head to look at her cast. "We were hoping for an encore, and now that we have it this cast has kindly agreed to sing this song with me for all of you. Please sing along if you know the words."

Marisa returned to her spot behind the piano, a place that felt as comfortable to her as any other spot ever did. Right before she put fingers to keyboard, she closed her eyes and said a prayer. "This is 'How Great Thou Art.'"

She began to sing, and then the cast on the stage joined in on the harmony one layer at a time until the song sounded robust and round. Out of the corner of her eye, she saw the audience, a few at a time at first, stand up and they began to sing along. Marisa believed that this was a night she would never forget. And to end on a song that was a part of her own Christmas tradition brought her to tears, tears that she didn't try to wipe away, tears that she didn't try to hide. These were tears of exhaustion, relief, pride and love. And she deserved to have them!

After the song ended, there was an odd lull as if everyone in the building had breathed in at the exact same time. Then, the room erupted with clapping that reached the rafters. Marisa went onstage, hugged Charity, and then held Charity's hand as the cast took one final bow and the curtain closed before them.

She couldn't move. She couldn't think. She couldn't do anything really other than stand like an old tree rooted to its place. It was done and it had been done well. The entire cast circled around her, linking arms and singing her praises. There would never be enough words to express to them how much they meant to her.

"All I can say is you are amazing artists and it has been my absolute privilege to know you, work with you and learn from you. Now let's go celebrate at The Library! My cousin Camilla is the owner and she's got a spread ready for us! We have damn well earned it!"

Dawson was standing next to his mom when Hannah Abernathy herself came to personally tell Mimi that Charity was the crown jewel of the show.

"Did you hear that, Randall?" Mimi whispered loudly enough that she really didn't need to attempt to whisper. "Our baby was the crown jewel!"

"Well," Randall said, his chest popped out with pride, "I think we already knew that."

"We did," Mimi agreed. "But it's nice to hear. Especially from an Abernathy!"

Once the curtain closed for the final time, all Dawson wanted to do was find Marisa and get her into his arms. That pretty red dress hugged her hourglass figure, and it had made all of his bells and whistles want to go off.

"Charity!" Mimi cried, reaching for her youngest child when she came off stage. "You were perfect. I've never been more proud of you."

Charity hugged her mom and then her dad and then worked her way down the sibling chain until she hugged Dawson.

"We had no idea you could sing like that, baby girl," Randall said, rocking back a bit on his heels.

"Well, all of the credit has to go to Marisa. She taught me so much in such a short amount of time."

Mimi's lips pursed and her body stiffened and she muttered something under her breath with a slight shake of the head.

Randall and Mimi wanted their triumphant daughter to join them at a party hosted by the Taylor family but Charity wanted to go to The Library with the rest of the cast to celebrate.

"Are you going to The Library with us?" she asked Dawson.

"That's a hell yes."

"Aren't you so proud of her?" She leaned over and asked for his ears only.

"Hell yes," he said again. "Do you know where she is?"

"She's outside speaking to a TV reporter. Everyone is hoping that after the extra publicity for Baby J his mother will come back to claim him."

After several more hugs from their parents, Charity and

he finally made it outside while Marisa was wrapping up her interview.

"Dawson?"

"Yes, baby sis?"

"Do you love her?"

Blindsided, Dawson looked over at Charity. "What kind of a question is that?"

"Do you love her?"

"I think so," he said, annoyed at the question in the first place.

"She's my friend."

"She's my friend too."

Charity bit her lip before she said, "Marisa isn't a... casual kind of woman."

"I know that."

"So...treat her like you would treat me. Respectful like."

"Charity, Marisa is not my sister. Gosh darn why did you just put that thought in my head!"

"That wasn't my plan, but if what I just said keeps you an honest man, then my work here is done."

The cast and crew of the Mistletoe Pageant, triumphant and high on good vibes and racing endorphins, gathered at The Library. They were loud and everyone seemed to be talking all at once. There was laughing, dancing, and there were times when groups of people began to sing, which prompted the rest of them to join in.

"You are amazing," Shira said as she found Marisa in the throng. "I've never seen anything like the show you just produced. TikTok is going to go crazy for you again."

Marisa hugged Shira tightly. Throughout the show, she relied on Shira to keep the beat and hold all of the instruments together.

"I can't thank you enough, Shira. You stopped your life to come to my rescue."

"That's what friends are for."

"Yes, but it's times like these that makes it crystal clear who are your friends and who are just acquaintances. And you, my dear, are the very best of friends."

"Same."

They linked arms together and walked in unison. "How do you like Bronco?" Marisa asked her friend.

"Handsome cowboys, bucolic views? What's not to love?"

"I've fallen in love with Bronco." Her personal truth? She had fallen in love with Bronco *and* Dawson John.

Shira linked arms with her. "Maybe we've both fallen in love with Bronco because we both fell in love with men *from* Bronco?"

"Maybe we shouldn't use the word *maybe*."

"That sounds like a song," Shira said. "Row House Four's first single. Maybe I can lure you back to Boston to play with us? We miss you."

"I miss you guys too," Marisa said. "But…"

"Your life is here."

"Yes."

"And now your love is here."

Marisa nodded still coming to grips with the depth of her feelings for Dawson.

Shira hugged her again and whispered in her ear, "Now go take advantage of that handsome cowboy."

Marisa blushed and laughed and hugged her friend one last time before returning to Dawson's side. After the cast and crew sang "For she's a jolly good lady," Marisa felt loved, appreciated and accepted by the Bronco community of singers, dancers and musicians, and it was better than she had hoped for when she first took this job.

"Your cousin throws a damn good shindig," Dawson said, seeming happier now that she had returned to him.

"She really does," Marisa agreed, then said, "I'm a little overheated. Take a walk with me?"

Dawson finished his beer, and then they walked out into the frigid air. He put his arm around her, drew her close to him and did his best to keep her warm.

"What's on your mind?" he asked her. "You seem like you're a million miles away from me."

She smiled up at him. "I'm not a million miles away from you. I'm just thinking about how grateful I am for you."

"For me? What did I do?"

"Everything, Dawson," she said. "You challenged me, you supported me, and pushed me to reach higher than I had ever thought to reach. I have always had confidence in my abilities. But seeing myself through your eyes? Your unwavering faith, your unwavering support, lifted me up when I could have easily missed a step and faltered. So, I'm grateful for that."

"If I managed to do all that for you, Marisa, then I feel as proud as a puffed-up peacock." His words made her laugh. "I want you to know that I'm grateful for *you*. You trusted me to help guide you. You made me think that if a woman as special as Marisa trusts me, then maybe I'm not just the black sheep of my family. Maybe there's more to me."

"You are much more than that, Dawson. Much more."

Dawson took in a deep breath and then he said, "I've got some mighty strong feelings for you, Marisa. Feelings that I've never felt before in my life."

Marisa felt a swell of emotions rising to the surface.

Even though she still couldn't see the road ahead that would bring them to the same place at the same time, Marisa wanted to savor every minute with Dawson she could.

"Do you remember when I told you that it was my turn to choose the next adventure?" she asked him.

"Yes," he said. "Lay it on me."

"Well, sex is considered to be a very good cardiovascular activity."

Dawson seemed to forget how to breathe and swallow. He started to cough and his eyes started to water.

"Are you okay?" she asked, patting him on the back.

"I don't know." He coughed a few more times. "That's really what you want to do?"

"You promised to do whatever I wanted."

Dawson grabbed her hand and started to head out for his truck. "Darlin', a deal is a deal. If sexy time is what you want, sexy time is what you're gonna get!"

Chapter Twelve

Dawson held her hand all the way out to their family ranch, the Double J. Marisa had been exposed to wealth like the Johns' during her time at Berklee. Being in those fancy Boston houses had always made her feel out of place and uncomfortable regardless of how nice the people inside of the houses were to her. It was internal for her—an unwanted insecurity that she had been unable to overcome. So, pulling onto the main road to the Double J started her stomach to churning.

The cattle ranches in Tenacity looked like working ranches—there was a good bit of rusty barbed wire from four decades back when the fence was first built, the wood on the fences and other buildings had turned a grayish brown and had bowed so much that it popped off the nail and separated from the other piece of wood. The buildings were old, with plenty of moss growing on the roofs. Weeds weren't bothered with because it was all hands on deck just to keep the place afloat. But the Double J? Even at night, the place was so lit up that she could see that every fence was freshly painted, with no bowed planks. The grounds were pristine, which meant that the Johns had plenty of money to hire landscapers. A job like that for a place of this size? Dawson's parents probably spent more money on ground maintenance than her parents made a year. Every building was built with a similar color pallet, and the ones she could see on the long, paved drive were in top-notch condition. All of these things taken together read as "money, money, money."

"It's beautiful," Marisa said with an audible waver in her voice.

"It is," he agreed. "The folks run a tight ship."

Dawson must have detected her nervousness because he reached over for her hand and squeezed it. "Are you sure you want to do this *here*?"

"We can't go to my aunt and uncle's house."

"True," he said. "What about a hotel?"

"So the clerk can sneak a picture of us and send it to the gossip column?"

"Good point. I started to earn my bad reputation back in high school. But I don't want to tarnish your good name."

"Thank you."

Dawson had slowed down while they hashed out their options. When he reached the inner sanctum gate, he stopped and didn't punch the code to open it.

"It's your decision, Marisa. Do we go forward or do we turn around?"

Marisa chewed the side of her nail for a second or two. "Will we run into your family?"

"My parents typically go to our mountain cabin for the weekends, so we won't run into them. But you may run into my siblings." He looked over at her, still holding her hand. "Is the risk one you're willing to take?"

Marisa took another quick moment to mull it over and in the end she said, "One hundred percent."

He kissed the back of her hand before he rolled down

his window, punched a code to open the gate so they could drive through.

Dawson parked his truck around the side where there was a side door to the farmhouse styled kitchen. Once inside the darkened kitchen, Dawson stopped at the refrigerator.

"Thirsty?" he asked.

"I could use a drink."

"Wine?"

"Yes, please. Red, sweet."

Dawson grabbed a bottle of wine and two glasses, then led her through the house to his room. A suite of rooms, actually.

Marisa walked around, taking it all in. "I think this bedroom is bigger than my childhood home!"

Dawson had stripped off his winter gear before he came over to help her out of her coat, hung it up next to his, and then gave her a bear hug. "Does that bother you?"

Marisa wished that it didn't but it did.

"I guess it does," she admitted.

Still hugging her from behind, Dawson kissed her cheek. "Is it a deal-breaker? Do I need to promise to give away every dime I have?"

Marisa pulled away. "Please don't make fun of me."

Dawson closed the distance she had put between them. He took her hands in his and looked deeply into her eyes so she could see his sincerity when he said, "Baby, I was teasing. I'm sorry if it came across that way. Forgive me?"

"Okay."

"Thank you." He kissed both of her hands, one right after the other. "Now, you said something about bed aerobics?"

That made her laugh, breaking the tension that had built up around them. "I did. Very good for our health."

Dawson got the party started by untucking his shirt, stripping it off and tossed it on a nearby chair.

"Holy cow," Marisa said. "It wasn't photoshop—your abs actually do look like that."

He smiled at her. "Why don't you come over here and inspect them. Touching is encouraged."

Marisa touched his six-pack abs, and she had never felt anything like that before. He was lean and muscular and so gosh darn beautiful that it took her breath away.

"I'm glad you finally took me up on my offer!" He laughed. "I was beginning to believe you'd never have the chance to inspect my best feature."

"Your abs are just one of many *best* features. Actually, let's just call your entire body your best feature!"

"So, you approve?"

"Me and the rest of the world."

"I don't give a damn about the rest of the world, Marisa. All I care about is you and me, in that bed, making love."

"Well, then, what are you waiting for, cowboy?"

"Not a damn thing," Dawson said. Then he swung her into his arms and carried her to bed.

Dawson held Marisa in his arms. All that he had imagined about making love with her had come true and then some. How could he have known what making love with a woman that had stolen his heart would be like? What he'd felt for the other women he'd dated—and there were quite a few—wasn't love as he felt it now. He had enjoyed those women and they had enjoyed him in a casual, no real attachment agreement. He hadn't misled anyone; he had never made empty promises. There had been a handful of women that he'd thought might have been a love connection. He knew now he had been wrong about that.

"Are you comfortable?" Dawson had his arm around Marisa's shoulders while she rested her head on his chest and her hand over his heart.

She made a languid, relaxed, happy noise in the back of her throat and curled herself even closer to him.

Dawson closed his eyes, kissed her on the top of her head and continued to stare up at the ceiling, his mind focused on the sensation of having Marisa so close to him. The feel of her silky thick hair on his naked flesh, the scent of her skin, the curve of her hips and the roundness of her breasts were intoxicating. One time hadn't been enough. He needed more, and then more, and then more. Her silky skin pressed against his was an aphrodisiac. Having his hard body enveloped by her softness and her warmth took his mind to a place so high above the clouds that he wondered if it was all a dream.

Marisa ran her finger along the ridges of his abdomen, and that sensation aroused him. He captured her hand and guided it down to the part of his body that seemed to need her the most.

"Again?"

"Get on top of me," he commanded, and he was grateful that she was so generous with her sweet body.

And then they were connected as one, her beautiful large, delectable breasts pressed against his hard chest, his hands holding her sumptuous hips as he rocked her back and forth. It was quiet this time, soft moans of pleasure, their breaths mingling. First was her pleasure and then it was his. Marisa's hands were on his shoulders, her hair was brushing over his arms and his chest, while she caught her breath. Dawson slowly rolled them both onto their sides as his body separated from hers.

"You're so beautiful," he whispered to her in the dark.

"*You* are so beautiful."

Marisa turned over so she could be the little spoon. Dawson listened while she fell asleep in his arms. And when her breathing was even and steady, he fell asleep, completely satiated from making love with an incredible woman who had just taught him the meaning, and the *feeling*, of genuine love.

Marisa awakened on the other side of the bed. Sometime during the night, she had turned and had cuddled with an amazingly fluffy pillow on Dawson's bed. It was nearly eight o'clock, and she couldn't believe she had made love to Dawson three times and then fallen asleep in his arms. No, she wasn't a virgin, but she wasn't a sex aficionado. Her experience was rather limited. Making love with Dawson, a man who had a very strong appetite, had made her feel incredibly sexy and desirable. But she wouldn't be honest with herself if she didn't have a small amount of regret. Not because she didn't want to make love with Dawson—she had and she did. What she regretted was the fact that she felt more connected and more attached to this incredible man. A connection that would make it very difficult to walk away from Dawson.

Maybe you don't have to walk away.

The tiny voice in her head gave her hope. Here, in the early morning hours, with Dawson sleeping beside her, she began to wonder if her negative assessment of their chances beyond this magical holiday season had been ill-conceived and a snap to judgment. Could she have a future with Dawson John? It seemed unlikely, but there was a sliver of hope now that hadn't been there before.

"Good morning," Dawson said in a sleepy voice as he reached for her.

"Good morning."

"How'd you sleep?"

"Like a baby." Marisa took her phone from the night-stand and saw that her aunt had responded to her text letting her know that she might be celebrating right through the night and into the early morning.

Dawson sat up. "I'm glad. Are you hungry?"

"I am," she said. "But I think I need to get to the the-ater, get my car, change out of these clothes so I can start packing up the props and costumes."

Dawson yawned, ruffled his hair, and then tossed the sheet off of his body and stood up, nude, without any self-consciousness at all. She pulled on her clothes from the night before that reminded her of the couple of times she had made the walk of shame. She hoped that Dawson had been right when he said that he doubted they would run into members of his family.

Dawson got dressed in jeans, T-shirt and boots. He walked over to Marisa, put his arms around her, kissed the top of her head and then kissed her lightly on the lips. "Are you sure you don't want me to scrounge up some breakfast for us here?"

"I am," she said. "I just don't want to—"

"I get it," he said. "I don't want to run into my family either."

Together they walked out of his suite of rooms and he took her back through the kitchen where he grabbed some fruit and small containers of orange juice for the road. Marisa followed him in her wrinkled dress.

They headed to his truck, got in, and when Dawson tried to turn over the engine, nothing happened.

"Damn." Dawson got out, lifted up the hood, fiddled with some wires and then tried to start it again.

"What's wrong?" she asked.

"I think it's the battery," he said. "Let's head over to the garage. We can borrow my mom's car."

Dawson typed in a code on a panel on the outside of the garage. The garage door opened and then it was too late. Inside, having just parked their Bentley in one of the bays, Randall and Mimi John were walking toward the door that would lead them into the house. Randall and Mimi stopped walking and so did they. Dawson cursed their luck under his breath, and all Marisa could do was stand there in broad daylight with "sex hair" and a disheveled dress that the Johns had seen her wear the night before.

"Dawson." Randall's one word held an encyclopedia of meaning.

"Dad," Dawson said. "Mom. You remember Marisa."

Mimi had a somewhat stiff in her eyes but she greeted Marisa and said, "You put on a lovely show, Marisa."

Feeling embarrassed, Marisa replied with a simple thank you.

But just when Marisa thought that this humiliating encounter was over, Mimi addressed her son. "Stop toying with her, Dawson. I don't believe this is a good match for either of you."

Having said that, Dawson's mother turned her back on them and disappeared into her mansion.

Randall shook his head back and forth, looking at the tips of his designer loafers. When he looked back up, he addressed Dawson only. "I'm not happy, Dawson. You're a man full grown, but as long as you live at the Double J, you need to abide by our wishes."

Marisa could feel the shift in Dawson's energy; she could see his jaw tighten, his eyes narrow, and every muscle in his body tense. But he remained quiet.

"I'm sorry it went this way, son, I really am." Randall gave a slight nod to her, and then he also went inside the house.

Dawson opened the passenger door of a forest green Jaguar and then got behind the driver's seat. He held his hands on the steering wheel with a tight grip and stared out of the windshield.

"I don't even know how to apologize to you about that."

It took Marisa a minute to gather her thoughts before she said, "I think that everything that needed to be said was said, Dawson."

Dawson had a grim look on his handsome face. "I don't know how I'm going to do it, Marisa. But somehow, someway, I'm going to make things right."

Even though she didn't blame Dawson for the rude, disrespectful, dismissive behavior of his parents, that didn't mean she wasn't taking an inventory of what their behavior meant for her relationship with Dawson. Perhaps this encounter with Randall and Mimi was a blessing in plain sight. This was a shot over the bow, and she couldn't stick her head in the sand and ignore the warning.

At the theater Dawson parked next to her car, which was covered in a dusting of snow from the night before. Dawson helped clean off her windshield and windows before he hugged her tightly and kissed her tenderly.

"What does this mean for us?" he asked her.

"Honestly, Dawson, I just don't know…"

"You don't know…" he repeated in a dull tone.

"I don't. I'm sorry. I still have to get myself packed up and on my way back to Tenacity. I'm the director and producer of our holiday show there, and I have a lot of work to do."

"When are you heading back?" he asked, his eyes shuttered, his arms crossed in front of his body.

"After Thanksgiving. I promised my aunt and uncle I'd help with the cooking. It's the least I can do."

"I'll let you go then," he said. "I'll call you later?"

She nodded. "Yes. Later."

"If you need my help packing up, I'm only a text away."

Marisa had the door open, one foot on the asphalt when she turned back to him, put her hand on his arm and said, "I don't blame you, Dawson. You aren't your parents' keeper."

"No, I'm not. But I'm sure as heck the one who's paying for their sins."

After Dawson dropped Marisa off at the theater, he drove back to the Double J without following any of the speed limit signs. He felt boxed in, controlled, like he wasn't his own man as long as he lived on the Double J and he couldn't stand it. It was their right to like or dislike whomever they wanted to, but to be so cold and rude to a woman he loved was his red line in the sand. And as far as following their rules while on Double J land, he could solve that problem right now. His parents wanted all of their children to marry and make a life at the Double J.

Dawson found his parents in the dining room having breakfast. He sat down at the table but didn't intend to break bread with his parents.

"Dawson, don't start," Randall said to him.

Mimi examined him. "I'm speechless Dawson. Is this some kind of adolescent rebellion?"

"The idea that you think it's okay to be rude to Marisa or anyone else I choose to spend my time with is crazy to me. What gives you the right?"

Randall's neck turned red. "I have every right. This is

still my ranch, Dawson. And as long as I'm breathing, I can say whatever I want, in any way I want, to whomever I want."

"Then I think it's time for me to move on."

"Suit yourself," his father said, and then went back to his paper.

Mimi made an audible gasp. "Now wait a minute. Let's all calm down. You aren't moving out, Dawson."

"Let him go," Randall said from behind the paper.

"No. We have always planned to have our children settle down on the Double J and raise our grandchildren right here with us," Mimi said before she asked, "What kind of hold does this woman have on you, Dawson? Is she worth losing your family—your home—over?"

"I love all of you. But, she's important to me, Mom." He pointed to his chest where his heart was housed. "In fact, she's the *most* important thing to me. And you hurt her. It's a deep cut that I'm not so sure will heal over."

"It's better to rip that Band-Aid off, Dawson." Mimi's tone shifted from cajoling to cold. "You don't see that now but I did her a favor. And I did you a favor."

Dawson shook his head feeling defeated that he couldn't get his mother to see how much he loved Marisa. "No, Mom, you didn't."

Randall crumpled the paper, put it on the table and slammed his hand on top of it. "That's enough."

Dawson gave a nod, pushed his chair back and stood up. "That's actually something we can agree on, Dad."

He passed Charity on the way out.

"What's wrong?" his sister asked.

"Ask them," he said, giving her a quick hug.

He'd had disagreements with his parents, but he'd never come close to leaving the family ranch. The ranch was in his blood—he loved the land and he wanted to contribute to the family legacy. But he loved Marisa. He *loved* Marisa. And the fact that his parents wouldn't accept her was sending him to a place mentally he'd never experienced before. He didn't want to burn any bridges with his family—even though he believed that Randall and Mimi were always too focused on appearances and keeping up with the Taylors and the Abernathys. Dawson loved his parents. But if he had to choose between the woman he loved and his family? He'd light a match and burn down the bridge and the whole damn house. That was his bottom line.

The day after her encounter with Dawson's parents, Marisa did her best to focus on packing up the theater. She felt grateful for the distraction because as much as she had tried to shield herself from hurt, her heart ached. She figured she wouldn't be the Johns' first choice for their son, but the blank stare Mimi had given her was actually more hurtful to her than if Dawson's mother had exhibited outright anger. At least there would have been a feeling in there somewhere. But the cold stare had sliced her down to the core of her being.

"Thank you so much for helping, Sam," she said to the carpenter who was helping her pack all of the decorations and larger set pieces that he had built for her. The plan was to load up all of them into a rental truck and the day after Thanksgiving, he was going to drive it to Tenacity and unload it for her.

"No problem," Sam said. "Happy to help."

While Sam continued to pack up the truck, Shira pulled her aside. "Are you okay?"

Marisa turned her head away, pressed her fingers in the corner of her eyes to stop more tears from falling. She had cried the night before and her eyes were puffy as a result. The rejection stung, of course it did, but it also shattered the slim hope in her heart that things might work out for her and Dawson. Family was too important to her; she would never marry a man whose parents didn't approve of her. That would set them up for a lifetime of pain, and she wouldn't put either of them in that position. So, as she had always suspected, this thing with Dawson could only ever be a holiday affair.

"No," she said to her friend, "I'm not okay."

Shira hugged her tightly and said, "I can see that something happened…"

"Yes. Something did happen. But I just…*can't* talk about it."

"I'm here for you, Marisa. You know that," Shira said. "No matter what, I'm in your corner."

"Thank you," she said, still fighting back another round of tears. "You're the best friend I've ever had."

Chapter Thirteen

The next day Dawson attended the opening of the Mistletoe Rodeo with his family. Things with his parents were still shaky after the incident, but their family tradition was to attend the rodeo together and that was a tradition that Dawson didn't want to throw away. Randall and Mimi would always be his parents, no matter what. And when he did eventually have children—and ever since he met Marisa, he'd been giving a lot of thought to the idea of having a family of his own—they would be his children's grandparents. Ever since he saw how emotional and caring Marisa was about Baby J, he had begun to see her in the light of a mother; and he could easily imagine her as his wife and the mother of his children. And he had to believe that given enough time, his parents would grow to love Marisa the way he loved her.

Charity, who was sitting next to him, skimmed the program while they were awaiting the opening ceremony that would kickoff the rodeo. A newcomer to the country music industry would be singing the "Star Spangled Banner." Charity leaned over and said to him, "Brooks Langtree, the Hawkins Sisters and Geoff Burris and his brothers Jack and Ross are all appearing today."

Dawson was preoccupied with his phone. He had called Marisa several times and she didn't pick up; he had also texted her and even though he could tell that she had read the text, she hadn't replied. She was avoiding him. The encounter with his parents at the Double J had done more damage than he originally thought.

"Damn," Dawson said under his breath. Part of him wanted to go find her and hash things out between them. But as much as he didn't care about appearances when his parents were trying to keep up with the Taylors and Abernathys, he didn't want to give the gossip mill more material when it came to Marisa and him. Everyone knew their family's tradition of going to the rodeo together. If he suddenly disappeared, folks who liked to share tidbits with the local gossip columnist would notice.

"What's going on?" Charity leaned over and whispered the question.

He shook his head, refusing to speak about it. He sent Charity a text instead, and when she read it, she looked over at him and frowned. He knew that Charity would share in his concern that Marisa wasn't communicating with him. Charity loved Marisa too.

"Why don't you get off your phone, little brother?" Maddox said. "There are some mighty fine women here who would make you a very happy man if you would just give them the time of day."

Not wanting to draw any more attention to himself, Dawson turned his phone on vibrate and put in the left pocket of his shirt just in case Marisa got back to him. Charity saw a friend on the bleachers down several steps; when she left, the seat between him and the aisle opened up. Before he could think anything about it, one of the daughters of a cattle family in a neighboring town, Emma Lou, appeared next to him. She was exactly the type of woman his mom wanted him to marry—cattle family pedigree and a debutante to boot. And of course he could see that she was pretty—everyone with eyes could. She had long blond hair, pretty blue eyes, fair skin, and a lean body from years of riding and playing hard with her older brothers. She was beautiful, bubbly and sweet as sugar. And she was uncomplicated. Before Marisa, Emma Lou might've made it onto the the short list of potential wives when he was ready to go that route further down the line. Mimi would have some reservations about the cost-benefit to their family in that Emma Lou's folks had half the land holdings and head of cattle.

"Hi, Dawson." Emma Lou sat real close.

Dawson tried to put some distance between him and her, but on his other side Maddox wasn't budging. Emma Lou came from a family that had been in Bronco for many generations. They didn't have money like the Taylors or Abernathys, or even the money his family had, but she did come from a family who had enough money to pass Mimi's litmus test.

"Hello, Emma Lou." Mimi leaned forward so she could greet his unwanted companion.

"Hi, Mrs. John! I hope you have a happy Thanksgiving."

"You too, dear." Mimi said with a smile. "Please tell your parents 'hi' from Randall and me."

"I will," Emma Lou said. "My parents just think the world of your family."

"Well, isn't that sweet?" Mimi smiled, "Don't be a stranger. You have an open invitation. I bet Dawson would just love to take you for a ride on the Double J."

Emma Lou glanced shyly at Dawson, a pretty blush on her cheeks. "I'd really like that. Thank you."

When his mother finished, Dawson said, "It's good to see you, Emma Lou."

"I couldn't believe it when I saw you sitting here," she said rather shyly, dipping her head down and looking at him from that angle. "I was actually hoping to see you here today."

"Is that right?"

She nodded. "I'm riding today during intermission. My riding team is part of the entertainment."

"Well, I'll be sure to watch out for you."

There was a lull in the conversation during which Dawson felt that Emma Lou had been angling for him to ask her out on a date.

"We're having a barbecue tonight to celebrate opening day of the rodeo. My mom and dad would love for you to come."

"I appreciate the offer, Emma Lou, but I'll have to take a rain check on that. I already made plans for this evening."

Emma Lou's full, glossy lips turned down into a sexy pout that Dawson was certain paved the way for her to get anything she wanted.

"He'd love to come," Maddox said as he leaned over.

Emma Lou looked between Maddox and him.

Dawson took his elbow and jammed it into Maddox's ribs. That made Maddox laugh while he rubbed his side.

"I'm sorry, Emma Lou," Dawson said, bent on saying the right thing to get Emma Lou off the bench and headed back to her seat. "I can't tonight, but maybe some other time."

Emma Lou brightened up, lost some of her shyness and she threw her arms around him, kissed him on the cheek, and then said, "I'd love a rain check! I'm going to hold you to it, Dawson John! And that ride on Double J."

After Emma Lou was out of earshot, Dawson snapped at his brother. "What the hell was that, Maddox?"

"Just helping you to move on."

"Well, damn well don't!"

Maddox held out his hands in surrender. "I hear you. I get it."

Dawson received a text, grabbed for his phone, looked at it and then shoved it back in his pocket. It was not Marisa.

"You're that hung up on this woman…"

"Marisa," Dawson said in exasperation. "Her name is Marisa."

"Okay," Maddox said, backtracking. "You're that hung up on Marisa."

"Yes. I am."

"You've picked a hard row to hoe, brother."

"That's my business, isn't it?"

Maddox nodded his head. "You're right. It is."

"Then back off."

"I'm just trying to help."

"If you want to help," Dawson said directly but not loud enough for their parents to hear over the din of the crowd, "when I do convince Marisa to marry me, accept her as I have accepted your wife."

Maddox looked stunned when he mentioned marrying Marisa in such stark terms. A moment later, he gave the slightest nod to let Dawson know he had heard him and had agreed to the terms.

He was tight with all of his siblings, but he wouldn't stand for their interference in his love life. His mood was dark and even the energy and excitement in the arena for the opening of the rodeo wasn't distraction enough. Why was Marisa refusing to answer his texts and voicemails? They had made love, and yes, had a horrible encounter with his parents, but he shouldn't have to pay for their sins. Marisa's behavior got him thinking—had his parents given her the out she needed to ghost him? Had this always been part of the equation for her? Have a holiday fling with a local cowboy and then move on? Had he misjudged Marisa that much?

To that last question, he answered "no." Marisa wasn't

the type of woman who had one-night stands on the regular. This undeniable bond between them went both ways. Maybe she didn't want to show it, but he had no doubt that she felt it just the same as he did.

Charity returned to her seat just in time for the opening of the rodeo. Riders carrying American flags galloped around the arena, and then they halted in a line on either side of a podium. The crowd was on its feet, stomping and yelling and hooting and hollering. And for a quick minute, Dawson's mind focused on the opening ceremony instead of fixating on Marisa.

"Good afternoon!" The mayor of Bronco stood on the platform. "Welcome to the Mistletoe Rodeo!"

That got another loud cheer from the crowd.

"Please remain standing for the 'Star Spangled Banner,' which will be performed by Miss Marisa Sanchez!"

Dawson's heart seized and his eyes found Marisa, dressed in jeans, boots, a Christmas sweater with blinking lights and a cowgirl hat.

"Marisa?" Charity asked, looking back through her program.

Marisa walked up the steps to the platform and accepted the microphone from Mayor Smith. A hush fell over the crowd, which made the unhappy grumbling of some spectators more noticeable to Dawson.

Marisa bowed her head for a moment before she began to sing the national anthem acapella. Marisa's clear, razor-sharp tone filled the stadium as she navigated the tricky parts of the national anthem seemingly without much effort at all. When she finished, the stadium erupted with clapping and cheers.

Dawson looked over and even his parents were clapping. Perhaps not as enthusiastically as most of the crowd, but they *were* clapping. That was a baby step.

Marisa took a bow and then waved to the crowd before she left the podium. Dawson kept standing and said to his parents, "You're proud of Charity's performance in the Mistletoe Pageant, Mom. Right?" He pointed to Marisa. "Well, Marisa's the one who saw her talent and helped her sing like an angel. Look, Mom, I love you. But I need you to see how special she is because I love her."

He'd made a scene and he didn't much care. Dawson didn't wait around to hear his parents' response. He scooted past Charity to the aisle, raced down the stadium steps and then ran to the area where the performers waited for their turn. Dawson ran into Sam backstage.

"Have you seen Marisa?"

"She just left," Sam told him.

"Which way?"

Sam pointed to the exit for the parking lot on the right side of the arena. If he could catch her, she couldn't ignore him like she could with calls or texts. He just needed to talk to her face-to-face; he was sure he could make her understand his parents and their family dynamic. Dawson took off toward the parking lot and then searched the rows of cars hoping to catch her before she left. He couldn't find her Falcon anywhere. He stopped running and paced in a circle while he caught his breath.

"Damn it!" Dawson cursed loudly. "Damn my rotten luck!"

Sheet music. Costumes. A few odds and odds. They were all that was left in the Bronco Theater for Marisa to pack. Sam had already loaded the larger items into the rental truck, and Marisa was all alone in the theater. She tried to focus on the task at hand, but her thoughts were elsewhere. With Dawson John.

When Marisa had been asked by Mayor Smith to sing the national anthem after the scheduled performer had come down with the flu, she had been happy to help. Standing up on the small stage, Marisa had known, that Dawson would certainly be somewhere in the crowd. She'd never thought that she would be able to pick him out of the densely populated stadium seats. It had been standing room only. But sure enough, she'd found him, and seeing him had made it difficult to sing. Her heart had been racing, her legs had gone weak at the knees, and it had taken every ounce of her self-determination to keep her focus on the lyrics. When she finished, she'd walked as quickly as she could to the back area, literally bumped into Sam as she rounded a corner and then headed out to the parking lot. She had been avoiding Dawson and she still was.

She wasn't proud of it but she was in self-preservation mode. Not only her heart but her work was at risk. The town of Tenacity was counting on her, and she refused to let her winter romance with Dawson John interfere with the preparations for the annual holiday show in Tenacity.

"Hello, sweetness and light." At the sound of the voice, Marisa looked up and saw Agnes enter the theater.

"Hi, Agnes."

Agnes looked at her closely. "You look heartbroken, Marisa."

Marisa's face crumbled as she turned toward Agnes and flung herself into the woman's arms. She had cried more in the last couple of days than she had in several years. She had fallen in love with Bronco and one of its native sons.

Agnes held on to her for a good long while before she asked, "Dawson?"

Marisa wiped her tears off of her cheeks with a nod.

"What happened?"

"I…" She paused, then restarted. "I spent the night at the Double J."

"Oh, I see."

"His parents returned early from their trip to the lake house…"

Agnes looked at her with years of wisdom in her eyes. "And it didn't go so well."

"No," Marisa said. "It didn't."

Agnes hugged her again before she asked, "And how has Dawson reacted to all of this? Was he supportive of you?"

"I heard from Charity that Dawson had a major blow up with his parents over me."

Agnes's bushy eyebrows lowered. "Charity told you? Not Dawson?"

Marisa shook her head. "I haven't spoken to Dawson."

"I see." Agnes rocked back on the heels of her sensible shoes.

Marisa began boxing some more items. "It's for the best."

"Maybe it is, maybe it isn't," her elder said slowly.

"We are too different, Agnes. We want different things. How we see our future is worlds apart."

"Fiddle sticks," Agnes said. "Finding your soulmate is the tricky part. Most people live their whole lives looking for their other half and never find it."

Marisa paused from her job and looked over at Agnes. "Were you one of those people?"

For the first time, she saw deep sadness in the elder woman's eyes. "No. I did find my soulmate."

"I didn't know you're married, Agnes. You've never mentioned it."

"I never married."

Marisa sensed that the story Agnes seemed to want to tell her deserved her full attention. "Why not?"

"Because I was young and I thought I had life all figured out," Agnes said. "Ben and I disagreed on just about everything. If I said the sky was blue, he'd say it was orange. If he said the grass was green, I'd tell him it was purple. The only thing we could agree on was that we loved each other. We were crazy for each other, much like you and your cowboy."

Marisa couldn't dispute that. She was crazy about her cowboy. But did Dawson *really* feel the same way about her? Or was he mistaking infatuation for love?

Agnes continued. "His parents didn't approve of me and mine weren't too thrilled either." She paused, swallowed several times, and then said, "We let the opinions of others dictate our relationship. And little by little, brick by brick, our relationship crumbled. Not our love," Agnes said emphatically. "Never our love."

"What happened to Ben?"

"He married a woman who passed whatever parent test I had managed to fail. He had several children."

"Oh, Agnes, I'm so sorry." Marisa hugged Agnes. "And you never married."

"No. I didn't," she said. "And there isn't a day that goes by that I don't feel regret. I hope you won't walk that same path, Marisa. It's a lonely one."

Dawson had almost given up trying to get in touch with Marisa; he didn't mind giving up some of his pride but not all of it. But then he received a text from her and he felt like he had just hit the lottery. Instead of texting her back, he called her.

"Hello?" Her voice was thin as she answered.

"Howdy, stranger." He tried to add humor to a situation that held no humor for him.

"Sorry."

"I need to see you, Marisa," he said seriously. "We need to talk."

"I agree."

"When?"

"Maybe the day after Thanksgiving?" she suggested. "I plan on leaving around noon."

"I was actually hoping you would stop by the Double J for Thanksgiving dessert."

There was a very long pause on the other end of the line.

"Dawson, your parents have made their feelings about me very clear," she said.

"And I have made *my* feelings about you very clear as well, haven't I?"

Another lengthy pause and Dawson silently cursed the fact he was doing the exact thing he hadn't wanted to do— get into a debate with Marisa.

"I understand how you feel, Marisa," he said, breaking the silence, "and I can't say that I blame you. But don't just shut me out of your life like we don't mean something special to each other. Please don't do that."

In his short experience with Marisa, he knew that she had a heart of gold—she was kind, considerate and did everything she could to make those around her feel good.

"Let's meet the day after Thanksgiving, say nine o'clock? At the theater?"

"Yes," she said. "Nine sharp. At the theater."

"Happy Thanksgiving, Marisa," he said, with a feeling of dread that Marisa may be trying to take then full circle and end their relationship exactly where it began.

"Happy Thanksgiving, Dawson."

Thanksgiving morning, Marisa was up early to prep all of the ingredients needed for the day. In the Sanchez household, the Thanksgiving menu always included traditional American dishes—turkey, stuffing, mashed potatoes and apple pie for dessert. But they also cooked dishes inspired by their Mexican heritage. Marisa's mother had taught her how to make fried polenta with chorizo, galletas de suero, roasted chile corn bread, chili lime Broccolini, pumpkin empanadas, and tres leches pumpkin flan.

Once all of the prepping was done, Marisa called her mom, dad and siblings in Tenacity to wish them a happy Thanksgiving. It was odd to miss Thanksgiving with her Tenacity family, but it was also a blessing to be spending a holiday with her aunt Denise, uncle Aaron and her cousins Dylan, Dante, Camilla, Sofia, and Felix and their significant others. The house was small and tidy, and the delicious smells from the kitchen made the entire house smell wonderful.

"Why so sad, Marisa?" Her great uncle Stanley appeared beside her while she made the pumpkin empanadas.

"I'm not sad," she said, and then she met Stanley's gaze and she realized that he had been on this earth too long to believe her flimsy attempt to pretend all was right in her world.

"Okay," she corrected, "I'm sad. But I'm doing my best to not let it ruin this special day."

"Did I tell you that Winona's daughter Daisy received a note from her?"

Marisa stopped her hands for a moment to give her great uncle her full attention. "No, you didn't."

"Well, she did. It said that she's fine and she just needed some space."

"Oh, Uncle Stanley, I'm sorry."

"Thank you," he said, and she could tell that while he was still heartbroken, the note confirmed everything he had ever thought about Winona—she was too independent to settle down with him.

"I think it's time for me to move on," he said. "But I just can't. I just—" he paused to gather his emotions "—can't. I love her too much. And I know she loves me. She could change her mind and if she does, I want to be waiting for her. I'm always going to wait for Winona."

Marisa gave him a hug, careful not to touch his shirt with her doughy hands. "I think she will find her way back to you, Tio."

"Thank you. I am glad to have an ally in love." Stan said, doing his best to regain his composure. "Now! Don't look so sad, dear one," her uncle said. "You never know who might show up at your door."

By noontime, the entire family, plus Shira and the carpenter, Sam, were migrating toward the tables. They were packed in tightly with card tables set up anywhere there was space, and Marisa absolutely loved it! The house was warm, redolent with the scent of Mexican spices, and there was loud laughter mixed with equally loud talking. The energy in the house was simply contagious, even for Marisa. She had awakened in a sad mood and missing Dawson, but the wonderful distraction of cooking for family had allowed her to feel joy in a holiday that had always symbolized the meaning of family for her.

A main table was set up, buffet style, and everyone got in line to take a turn. It made Marisa feel a sense of satisfaction to see her family and friends fill their plates full with the food she had helped to prepare. Marisa was ready to get into the line when she heard a knock at the door. Stanley answered it, and then she heard him say, "Dawson John! Happy Thanksgiving!"

Marisa's heart jumped into her throat, and she froze like a deer in headlights. She peeked around the corner, certain she hadn't heard what she thought she heard. There, standing in the doorway holding a pie in his hands, was Dawson. Now she understood the cryptic comment her great-uncle had said about someone showing up on their doorstep!

"Happy Thanksgiving, Mr. Sanchez. Thank you for inviting me," Dawson said. "I have this pie for you, but I didn't make it."

"Mr. Sanchez is my father," Stanley said. "Call me Stan."

"All right, Stan." Dawson crossed the threshold. "This pie was made by your neighbor. She caught me on the sidewalk and asked me to give it to you specifically. Seems to me she's trying to win your heart."

Stanley looked at the pie as if he was trying to offer him a poisonous snake. The elder gentleman simply refused to take it off his hands.

"Well, Dawson," Stanley said, "The quickest way to a man's heart is though the stomach. And, I did tell her that my favorite pie is cherry. I never get to eat cherry pie on Thanksgiving. Majority rules so it's apple pie or pumpkin pie for me."

"Not this year."

Stan gave him a brief smile and welcomed him inside, still refusing to physically take the pie. "You're correct young man! Not this year. Perhaps this pie is a sign that it *is* time for me to get back in the saddle."

"Well, Stan, that is a mighty fine looking pie."

When her great-uncle put his arm around Dawson's shoulders and patted him on the back like they were very old pals, Marisa felt all bent out of shape. She didn't even know that they two of them were acquainted at all much less her great-uncle inviting the man that she was currently trying to avoid to Thanksgiving dinner!

Chapter Fourteen

"**M**arisa!" Great-Uncle Stanley called out for her. "Look who I just found at the door! And he comes bearing a gift!"

Marisa met Dawson in the small foyer with a forced smile on her face and a cheerfulness in her voice while her family watched them curiously. "Well, Dawson John! What a surprise! Happy Thanksgiving."

He smiled at her like he had just pulled off the most amazing trick. "Why thank you, Marisa. Happy Thanksgiving to you too!"

"Let me take that pie off your hands," she said to avoid any attempt on his part to hug it out. But if she were being completely honest, she also needed an excuse to make use of her hands so she didn't leap into his very strong, very hard-muscled arms. She didn't think there was a chance for them to achieve long-term happiness together, but her body had a mind of its own. Her body wanted to find a private place ASAP so she could strip the cowboy out of his expensive clothing and take him for a nice long ride. She was blushing just thinking about it!

Her aunt came over to welcome Dawson. "What a wonderful surprise, Dawson."

Dawson smiled at Denise. "I was happy to get the invitation from Stan. I hope it isn't too much trouble."

"It's no trouble at all! Please make yourself comfortable." Denise pointed to a laden down chair in the foyer. "Coat pile's over there." Then she turned to Marisa. "Let me take that pie off your hands so you can spend some time with your beau."

"He's not my beau," Marisa said in a harsh whisper.

"Well, I suppose that's an old-fashioned word." Denise seemed to miss the point. "Love interest? Boyfriend? Your plus-one?"

"Don't you have to get that pie to the dessert table?" she asked, praying to a higher power to make this conversation end.

"Yes! Lord if my head wasn't attached!" Aunt Denise said good-naturedly. "And you might sit down for a spell, Marisa. Your face is red as a hot coal in a firepit."

Marisa cringed and then glanced over her shoulder to see if Dawson had heard that. He had.

"Surprise?" he said with a sheepish expression on his face.

"What are you doing here?" she asked under her breath while she pressed her cool hands onto her neck and cheeks. "We agreed to see each other tomorrow…"

"Yes. Nine sharp. I'll be there with mistletoe." He smiled that smile of his that made it difficult to concentrate much less stay angry with him. "But I didn't want to be rude to Stan by turning him down. He's been through a lot lately what with the note Daisy received from her mother. So, when I ran into him at the hardware store—"

"The hardware store? Why were *you* there?"

"I'm a rancher, Marisa, which means that I do ranch work." He held out his hand for her to inspect. "Look here. These are the calluses of a man who works with his hands."

"Those could just as easily be from pulling handles of

slot machines in Vegas," she said, resisting the urge to fold her arms in front of her body. "You aren't the only sleuth on social media."

He then leaned down to say for her ears only to hear, "Now I am kind of offended because I thought you would have felt these calluses when I touched every inch of your sweet, sexy, succulent—"

"Dawson!" She said his name while looking around for any prying ears.

"—body."

Marisa wanted to grab his overpriced designer cashmere coat off the pile on the couch, march back over to him, throw it at him and then escort him to the front door, push him out on the stoop and then laugh triumphantly as she slammed the door in his face.

But she did none of that. Instead, she led him into the living room where he knew Shira and Sam were talking with her cousins.

"Dawson!" The room erupted with good cheer when Dawson entered the room. With his height and those ridiculously broad shoulders, Dawson seemed to make the cozy room shrink. While everyone made a big fuss over him, she did her best to appear perfectly normal on the inside while she felt absolutely and positively *not* normal on the inside.

She entered the kitchen, ran the gauntlet of relatives looking at her with hopeful, romantic eyes before she reached her great-uncle, who she asked in the softest, most pleasant voice she could manage at that point in time, "May I have a word with you, Uncle Stanley?"

"Well, sure I have a minute for you!" Great-Uncle Stanley said in a booming voice that made everyone in the kitchen look over at them. "Is there something wrong?"

"No! No, no. Nothing's wrong," she was quick to say

with an equally quick smile to her relatives. "I'd just like some advice."

Still with a smile on her face, which stayed in place until she was out of view, she led her great-uncle to the guest room she had been occupying. She waved him in before shutting the door.

"Why did you invite Dawson for Thanksgiving?" she asked in a frustrated, yet still respectful whisper.

"Well, I saw that you were looking a little down in the mouth and since today is all about gratitude and forgiveness, and since I figured the two of you must have had a lovers' spat when I ran into him at the hardware store, I invited him. Aren't you happy to see him?"

"It's a mixed bag," she said honestly. "Why didn't you ask me first? And how do you know Dawson anyway?"

"Well, I believe I met him at a town picnic. He's very friendly," Stanley said. "And I didn't ask you because I thought that it would be a nice surprise for you."

Marisa closed her eyes tightly, working very hard to keep calm. In the interim, her great-uncle asked, "Are we all good? Dinner is about to begin and I want to get out there before the kids scrape all of the marshmallows off of the sweet potato casserole."

"Well, I can't blame you there. I've got a soft spot for marshmallows too," she said. "But just for future reference, Uncle Stanley, I loathe surprises!"

Stanley tapped the side of his head with his finger. "I've got that little tidbit locked in right up here."

"Okay." She couldn't stay mad at Uncle Stanley so she just gave up trying. He meant well, she knew that. And since she couldn't go back in time and stop the hardware store event, she was just going to enjoy the holiday. Dawson was, in fact, here so she had to believe it was simply meant to be.

When she walked into the kitchen, it was almost empty—only Aunt Denise was still there. In the living room, a crowd had gathered around Dawson as if he was a rock star or famous actor. The women were fawning and the men were laughing and slapping him on the back.

Hands on her hips, she asked, "What is it about that man?"

Aunt Denise kept on arranging the buffet but she looked over and asked her, "I think you might be able to answer your own question, *sobrinita*."

When Uncle Aaron announced, once again, that it was time to eat, everyone lined up to fill their plates with Great-Uncle Stanley first to the "sides" table.

"This is a plot twist," Shira said as she jumped the line with the blessing of those behind her. She came up close to Marisa.

"Isn't it though?"

Dawson, who had already managed to fill his plate, stopped chewing for a split second, smiled at her, gave her a thumbs-up and then went right back to chewing.

"Did you know…?" Shira asked.

"Uncle Stanley," she said. "He wanted to surprise me."

Shira laughed. "Mission accomplished."

Marisa narrowed her eyes in thought. "I've only known Dawson for a hot minute, but I think there is more to this invitation than meets the eye."

"Fishy." Shira nodded.

After they both scored their food, Shira and she took their seats at the card table where Sam and Dawson had already nearly cleaned their plates.

"Ladies." Dawson and Sam both stood up and held out the chairs for them.

"How's the food?" Marisa put her napkin in her lap.

"I've never tasted anything this good." Dawson stabbed at an empanada.

"I second that," Sam said, scooping up a big helping of garlic mashed potatoes.

"How did you manage to beat us to the table?" she asked.

"Everyone is so sweet here," Dawson said with a happy grin on his face. "They asked us what we wanted and they brought it to us."

"Of course they did," Marisa said in resignation.

"Now," Dawson said after cleaning his plate, "I didn't expect to see you here, Sam. That's been a nice surprise."

"Good food. Good company." Sam smiled at Shira before he hopped back in line for a second go-round.

Dawson pat his stomach. "Well, she isn't quite full yet. I think I can go for seconds myself. Can I get you anything while I'm up?"

"No. Thank you," she said with a small smile.

"Go in hot," Sam told him. "I had to fight for this last empanada. The Sanchezes don't play."

"Wish me luck." Dawson pushed back from the table.

"Godspeed, noble knight!" Sam held out his fork for Dawson to clink with his fork.

When Dawson came back with another full plate, Aunt Denise and Uncle Aaron began a time-honored tradition of having each guest saying what they were grateful for. This was one of her favorite parts of the holiday and when it was her turn, she knew exactly what she wanted to say.

"I am grateful for my faith and for my big, beautiful, Sanchez family. Thank you for all of the support you have given me over the years. I am thankful for Agnes Little and all of her guidance during the preparation for the Mistletoe Pageant. And I am thankful for my friends Shira and Sam who were pillars of strength when I was off my rocker. And I feel very thankful for Charity John who is an incredible talent, and I now feel very lucky to call her my friend."

She hadn't known until this very moment how she was going to handle the Dawson *situation* but then, after looking into his ocean blue eyes and seeing a part of him that was as trusting and hopeful as one of her students back in Tenacity, Marisa decided to just speak from her heart. "And last but certainly not least, I am thankful for you, Dawson. You helped me understand Bronco and pulled me out of a nosedive. You were the secret ingredient of my success."

One of her male cousins cupped his hands around his mouth and said, "I'll be grateful when Marisa is done being thankful!"

Everyone laughed and she said, "Whoever said that? No dessert!"

Dawson stood up and said, "I am thankful for friends, family, my health, and the Sanchez family for inviting me in and feeding me so well."

When he patted his stomach, her relatives laughed along with him. Dawson just waltzed in, as he always did, with his good looks and cowboy charm and just won everyone over!

"But what I am most thankful for is Marisa." Dawson caught her gaze and held it. "You taught me what true love is and what true love means to me. So thank you, Marisa. I love you."

While her family and friends burst out with clapping and hooting and making kissing noises to tease her, Marisa felt like her entire being got blown backward. Dawson confessed his love for her in front of her entire Bronco family! The room went quiet and fuzzy in her mind and there was an odd ringing in her ears and she felt just a bit nauseous. This was the "sickness" Agnes had said was going around the theater. Not the flu or the common cold—it was *love*! And she had been bitten by that bug and had come down with a very strong case of love for Dawson John.

After clearing off the tables to make room for dessert, Marisa asked if her aunt Denise needed anything.

"Not at the moment, *sobrinita*," Denise said. "Why don't you keep Dawson company. It was such a nice surprise that he accepted Uncle Stanley's invitation! He's a good one."

Marisa decided that it would be helpful to have a private confab with Dawson and probe him about how this invitation came about.

"Dawson?" She found him in the living room sitting on the couch sandwiched in between two of her cousins while he watched the football game in Spanish.

"Yes, my love?"

"I'd like to take a stroll," she said. "Care to join me?"

"It'd be my pleasure and my honor."

They passed Shira on their way to the front door. "I'll save you some rugalach."

"Thank you," Dawson said. "I had my eye on that."

"Not for you dummy," Shira said.

Dawson exaggerated a hurt look. "It's Thanksgiving, Shira. Aren't you supposed to be extra nice to people?"

Shira turned around, her thick curls bouncing around her shoulders. "I'm sorry, Dawson. Let me try again and give you some friendly advice. If I were you, I'd consider wearing a helmet."

Dawson's chance meeting with Stanley wasn't by chance at all. He knew several people who worked in establishments along Commercial Street who knew Stanley's morning route. First, Stan grabbed a cup of coffee, black, and then he bought the newspaper, tucked it under his arm, and then right before he reached the hardware store, he threw his empty cup of coffee into the garbage can and then walked into the hardware store, newspaper still tucked tightly under his left arm. The owner of the hardware store, the father of one of the boys Dawson played high school football with, didn't mind giving him the 411 on Stanley's route and he "bumped" into Stanley, a man savvy to the ways of the heart and, after expressing his heartache about not sharing a special holiday with Marisa, he had managed to finagle an invite to the Sanchez Thanksgiving.

"I'm glad you enjoyed dinner with my family," Marisa said quietly.

He had offered her his arm and was heartened that she took it.

"It's the best Thanksgiving meal I've ever had," he said honestly. "Thank you for not tossing me out on my ear."

"Don't think I didn't consider it." She laughed, enjoying the smoke curls that appeared for a short time when she spoke.

"Oh, I bet you did," he said. "What changed your mind?"

"Thanksgiving." She paused, then said, "You."

Dawson stopped walking and looked down at Marisa's lovely face. "Hold up. Am I about to receive some sort of credit for something?"

"Pump the breaks, Dawson." She favored him with a small smile. "You won't be receiving a medal of honor anytime soon."

"Darn it."

"But I could see how much you wanted to be with my family…"

"You."

"My family and me. So I decided, in the spirit of Thanksgiving, to forgive you for whatever you did to get Great-Uncle Stanley to invite you."

He started walking again and tried to think of some rational way to explain the invitation but couldn't think of anything other than some version of the truth. "Well, I did bump into Stan in the hardware store. But I wouldn't be telling the whole truth if I said it was accidental."

"Go on…"

"I planned it," he admitted. "I had some folks help me figure out his routine and—" he shrugged "—I bumped into him on purpose."

Marisa looked up at him with a disapproving eye. "And how did you manage to get my great-uncle to invite you?"

"Actually, he kind of did it on his own."

Marisa shook her head.

"Hear me out," Dawson said. "I did plan the meetup, but I was just hoping that he would put in a good word for me with you. But then he started to tell me that you were missing me…"

"He did not!"

"…and I told him how much I was missing you. And I think he took pity on me, Marisa. Stan is a man who understands how a broken heart feels."

Marisa turned around to head back to the house. "It wasn't his place to tell you that I was…missing you."

"He was just trying to be helpful," Dawson said. "Don't be mad at him."

"I'm not. How could I be? He's nursing a broken heart and he doesn't want anyone else to feel that pain."

Slowly, they walked together, and Dawson felt like a

lucky man when Marisa moved closer as small flakes of snow fell from the sky.

"Was Stan right? Were you missing me?"

Marisa didn't answer right away; she took her time while he suffered in the silence.

"Of course I missed you," she finally admitted. "But I thought it was best if we spent some time apart to clear our heads and process what has happened...between us."

She looked up at him with those brown eyes that were soulful and sexy, eyes he wanted to look into for every single day of his life. There was no question. He was convinced that Marisa Sanchez was his one true love.

"It *has* been a whirlwind," she added after a step or two.

"Most epic love stories start that way," Dawson replied. "And as for time apart, I couldn't disagree more."

Marisa raised her eyebrows at him, doubting his words. "So are you now an expert on love, Dawson?"

"Now that I've met you? Yes," he said definitively. "You leave tomorrow, and I have no idea where we stand and that *not knowing* is driving me nuts. I love you and I believe in my heart that you love me too! We don't need less time, *mi corazon*." In the yellow light of the streetlamp, he could see it on her face that he had surprised her in a good way when he called her "my heart" in Spanish. "We need a lifetime of time."

Chapter Fifteen

Declaring his love for Marisa when he knew darn well that she might just reject him and leave him heartbroken for the first time in his life scared Dawson in a way that he couldn't possibly explain or express. All he knew was that climbing up rock faces at high altitude, BASE jumping off of bridges, skydiving, any other adrenaline-spiking things that he had done all of his life—*none* of those things compared to the fear he had at the thought that he might lose Marisa forever. Once she went home and got settled back into her life—a life she didn't think he could live with her—they would lose all momentum and he would become a small blip on Marisa's lifeline. Perhaps a fond memory eclipsed by this imaginary perfect man she had in her mind. He *had to* convince her to think with her heart, not her mind.

He stopped walking to take her hands into his as snowflakes swirled around them in a magical dance. "I never expected this, Marisa. I've felt more, said more, stood up for what *I* want more than I ever have in my life. I've grown leaps and bounds because of my love for you. I mean, heck, I declared my love for you in front of *everyone* like a lovesick puppy."

She smiled at him. "It was the highlight of the Thanksgiving *'What are you thankful for'* Sanchez family tradition."

"See there?" Dawson said. "Old Dawson…"

"Three-weeks-ago Dawson."

"…would never have done something like that. *Never!* That's got to count for something, don't you think?"

She didn't answer right away but finally said, "I don't know what to say…"

"I only want you to say what's in your heart, Marisa. Nothing more, nothing less."

Quietly, thoughtfully, Marisa said to him, "Dawson, you were a complete surprise for me."

"Yes, I know. And you for me!" he told her. "I sounded like a first-rate sap in front of your entire family! Ever since the day that I met you, I've been asking, *Who the heck are you, dude?*"

"You didn't come off any way other than sincere," Marisa said. "You spoke from your heart. That's what you want from me, which is no less than what you have given to me tonight."

Then she added, "And, *of course*, my family adores you!"

That made him smile because that was a major win in his column. "They do, don't they?"

"People cannot resist you," she said with a resigned sigh. "My friends, my family. Anyone with a pulse."

"How about you?" Dawson asked in a deliberately flirtatious manner. "Can *you* resist me?"

Dawson smiled at her with his brilliant, charming smile, the smile that reached his blue eyes that changed from light blue-gray to an enigmatic ocean blue depending on the light. Factor in the perfect chin, strong nose and jawline that were sheer perfection no matter the angle, and Dawson became the stuff of photographers' dreams! Add to all of that his body by Greek gods and his confidence… Dawson was pushing the boundaries of what it meant to be human.

"Ugh," she said with an eye roll. "You're so annoying with all of those pretty boy good looks and cowboy charm."

"You are the very first complaint I have ever had," he countered.

"Nauseating."

Dawson laughed good-naturedly. "You look like you need a kiss."

"I'm not going to kiss you in front of God, my friends and my family."

"We could duck around the side of the house where it's dark. I've already spotted a couple of places where no one can to see us."

"First, you're giving of a stalker vibe," she said as they continued on the short walk to her aunt and uncle's house. "Second, I think we should steer clear of any *romantically driven* activities."

"Making love?"

She nodded and then shook her head and the sultry way he said "making love" made every fantasy come to life in her mind.

In a whisper, she said, "Yes. That. Keep your voice down…"

"So no kissing?"

"No! Absolutely not," she said as she pointed to the house. "We are going to go inside that house, act like civilized people…"

"No problem."

"*And* we are going to table any serious or potentially emotional topics until tomorrow."

"Don't worry," he said with a cavalier shrug. "We've already established that your family loves me."

She stopped and looked up at him when they reached the front door. "Dawson?"

"Yes, *mi corazón*?"

"Sometimes I feel like slugging you right in the arm!"

"Oooh." Dawson wiggled his eyebrows at her with a chuckle. "Foreplay."

"This was such a wonderful Thanksgiving," Aunt Denise said.

The majority of the family had headed home while Marisa helped her aunt clean up the kitchen and put away the leftovers. And even though she had spent Thanksgiving in Bronco instead of Tenacity, it had been a memorable holiday. One full of surprises. She certainly hadn't expected to see Dawson at their front door. She'd been thinking of him ever since he'd left. While her heart rejoiced at seeing him, walking with him, wrapping her arm in his, her practical mind just could not piece together a long-term future with him. If she couldn't see a "forever" with Dawson, wouldn't it be easier on them to make a clean break when she left for Tenacity tomorrow?

She didn't know the answer to that question yet. All she knew was that she'd get no sleep tonight as she mulled it over.

She focused on her aunt. "Yes, it was a wonderful Thanksgiving," Marisa agreed.

Many of the family members would be back tomorrow to eat again—everyone knew the food was even better the next day. In fact, she planned on leaving Bronco at noon the next day so she could share Thanksgiving leftovers with her parents and siblings in Tenacity. But first she had to meet

Dawson at the theater and Marisa was dreading it. She truly loved Dawson. They loved each other. But even though it was said in songs and repeated for generations of hopeless romantics, love couldn't conquer all. It just couldn't.

"I was so happy to have Dawson with us," Aunt Denise said. "He's such a nice young man. Polite. Considerate. And so handsome. It's hard to believe that any one person could be that handsome, but then there he is! Living proof."

"He is handsome."

"And just imagine! Dawson John in love with my niece." Aunt Denise beamed at her. "The two of you could make the most beautiful babies!"

Marisa froze. "Aunt Denise, we just met! I live in Tenacity and he lives in Bronco."

"Oh, please," her aunt said. "Those are molehills."

"By the way," Denise said, "did you hear that Dottie is fostering Baby J?"

Marisa stopped her work and looked at her aunt. "No. I didn't! I'm so glad you told me. Baby J broke my heart."

"I think he broke every heart in Bronco."

Still wired by too many cups of coffee, Marisa kept working on the stack of plates, and out of the corner of her eye, she saw Great-Uncle Stanley heading toward the front door spruced up with a button-down shirt and a tie.

"Where are you going all dressed up?" Marisa called to him.

With a sheepish look on his face, Stanley backed up, poked his head in to the kitchen and said, "I thought I'd go next door and thank our nice neighbor for the delicious cherry pie."

"What a wonderful idea, Uncle Stanley!" Aunt Denise exclaimed. "Ask her if she'd like to come over tomorrow. Plenty of leftovers."

Stanley acted excited by the idea, but that excitement, Marisa noticed, did not reach his eyes. "You never know. I just might."

Marisa walked over to him and fiddled with the tie knot. "There you go. That's better."

"You are a dear," Stanley said.

"Tio," she said in a lowered voice for only their ears, "you haven't eaten one piece of that cherry pie."

"I didn't?" Stanley didn't make eye contact, fiddling with his tie. "Just an oversight, I'm sure."

Everyone in the family wanted to see Stanley happy again after his broken engagement with Winona. A nice neighbor who baked his favorite pie just might be a new love interest that would serve to heal Stanley's bruised heart. But, from Marisa's vantage, Stanley didn't look like a man ready to move on. In fact, Marisa was convinced that he never would be no matter how many well-meaning friends and relatives wanted him to.

As Stanley left, Shira appeared balancing a stack of plates and cups and balled-up napkins.

"I think the living room is in pretty good shape now," her friend said.

"Thank you!" Aunt Denise had taken a liking to Shira. "You didn't have to do that!"

"And you didn't have to feed me."

"Fair enough." Denise flashed a tired smile. "I'm about to call it quits with this mess."

"I'll finish washing," Marisa said.

Her aunt hugged her tightly with tears in her eyes. "I'm going to miss you, Marisa. I'm used to you being with us now."

"I'll be back," Marisa said. "I promise."

"I'm going to hold you to that," she said, and then hugged Shira. "You come back too, you hear?"

"Yes, ma'am."

Aunt Denise shuffled off to bed and in what seemed like no time at all, Stanley returned and his head was down, and she could see tears on his cheeks. She went to him, "Tio, what happened?"

Stanley accepted her hug and whispered, "I went right up to her door and I stood there and stood there and," he paused, "I just couldn't do it. I couldn't. So I came home."

"I'm so sorry, Tio."

He wiped the tears for his love off his cheek with a hand-kerchief Marisa knew Winona had accidentally left with him. "I couldn't eat that pie, Marisa. Not one slice. If I did, I would feel disloyal to Winona."

"You don't have to eat the pie, Tio."

"I'm not going to." Stanley shook his head. He kissed her on the cheek and disappeared down the hallway. Feeling sad for her uncle, Marisa went back to her cleaning, and then her mind wandered as it often did to Dawson. She could see some of her uncle's traits in him; he loved quick, he loved hard, and he was hard to move once he had given a woman his heart. Could she learn from Uncle Stanley's and Winona's romance or was this, in truth, a cautionary tale.

Marisa pushed herself to finish the kitchen chores with Shira's help. When they were done, the kitchen was back in order and all of the food was safely stored in the refrigerator for tomorrow's post-Thanksgiving meal.

"I'm beat," Shira said, slumping onto the couch with a glass of wine in her hand.

"Me too," Marisa said. "Exhausting and yet totally worth it."

Shira nodded and they stopped talking for a bit and enjoyed the silence. Marisa's mind was whirling. Tomorrow she would be leaving Bronco. And that meant she was leaving Dawson too.

"So, tell me." Shira turned her body toward Marisa. "What's going on? Dawson crashed Thanksgiving?"

"Yes, he did."

"Why?"

"He was afraid to let time pass after..." Marisa didn't like to think about the scene with Dawson's parents much less give voice to it.

"After what?"

Marisa recounted the scene at the Double J and Mimi's blatant rejection of her.

Shira stared at her for a moment before she shook her head in disbelief and wordlessly got up, sat down next to her and wrapped her arms around her.

"I am so sorry, Marisa," Shira said to her. "You didn't deserve that."

Shira didn't move back to her spot at the other end of the couch; instead, she stayed close, holding her hand.

"I've never felt that humiliated in my life," Marisa admitted. A long-term relationship always felt like a long shot at best, but after Mimi's rejection, that long shot became an impossible shot. She felt sure of it now.

Shira squeezed her hand to comfort her. "And what did Dawson say about it?"

"He was furious," Marisa said. "And from what I heard from his sister, Dawson had a heated argument with his parents."

"He's protective of you."

"Yes, he is. And I feel protective of him."

"What do you mean?"

"Family is everything to me," she said. "I will not be the reason Dawson cuts his parents out of his life."

"Would he actually do that?"

"Yes," Marisa said quietly, "I believe he would. He loves me."

"And you love him?"

"I do. And I would never marry a man whose family doesn't accept me. Even if we *could* work through our differences, Mimi John's disapproval is a deal-breaker for me. No matter what, those are his parents, his flesh and blood. Dawson will always be stuck in the middle, unable to choose between his mother and his wife and never be able to completely please either of us. And when the children come, and they would most certainly come, will Mimi John accept them? There are just too many *what-ifs*, and when I add them all up, it's…"

Shira nodded her understanding and filled in the last two words of that sentence. "Game over."

The morning after Thanksgiving was overcast, windy and cold, with a few snow flurries swirling around in the frosty air. Sam was on the road to Tenacity with the sets and props. Shira had left early to catch a flight back home and Marisa already missed her dear friend. She had just packed her suitcase and put it in the trunk of her car along with a container full of the last chocolate rugalach, before she said a final goodbye to her aunt, uncle, and great-uncle Stanley.

"Couldn't you stay longer?" Aunt Denise asked one last time.

"I wish I could, but I have to get back to Tenacity and begin to prepare for that holiday show."

"I understand." Aunt Denise gave her one final hug and a kiss on the cheek. "I love you."

"I love you."

Stanley took charge of her suitcase and walked out to the car with her, and then hoisted the suitcase into her truck.

"I hope you have a wonderful time on your date."

"I will! All I have to do is turn on that Sanchez charm," Stanley said with a wink.

"True," she said, walking to the driver's-side door.

But Stanley blocked the door and asked, "So, what happened with that beau of yours?"

"Nothing to report. He had a good time and we left it at that."

"Don't give up on him, Marisa. Don't do that," Stanley said with a direct gaze. "He has such a deep love for you. I can see it in his eyes as plain as day."

She really didn't want to dredge up things that she had been actively trying to bury and forget. But Stanley was her elder and she had to show him that respect. "Sometimes love isn't enough."

Stanley threw up his arms and exclaimed, "What do you mean love isn't enough!"

Marisa wanted to point out that he was currently nursing a wound to the heart from Winona, but she would never rub salt into a wound and kept that point to herself.

Instead, she replied, "Dawson and I are so different. I think if I tallied everything up, we would have more in the different column than in the in-common column."

"Well, that's your problem right there, *mi gran sobrina*! Don't tally! In fact, *never* tally! I had a very successful marriage to my beloved first wife, and do you know the secret of that marriage?"

"Don't tally?"

"*Never* tally!" Stanley hugged her again.

"Okay, *gran tio*, I will try," she said and then added, "Tio! Don't give up on Winona."

"I won't. No. I won't!" her uncle called after her. Just before she got behind the wheel, Stanley blew her a kiss and she blew on back and he caught it and put it on top of his heart.

On her way to the theater, Marisa was mulling over everything that had happened in the whirlwind that was her time in Bronco. She felt like she needed weeks to process the events, and she still had conflicting thoughts in her affair of the heart with Dawson. Halfway to the theater, Charity John called.

"Hi, Charity!" Marisa said, happy to hear from her new friend and also happy for the distraction.

"Did I catch you at a bad time?"

"No. I'm just heading to the theater to make sure I haven't left anything behind. I also have to say goodbye to Agnes. I hate goodbyes, and I've already had too many today."

"I'm not looking forward to you being back in Tenacity," Charity said. "I already miss you."

"I miss you too," Marisa said. "But we're only an hour and a half away. You're always welcome to visit me. My couch is a pullout."

"You might be sorry. I might just take you up on that."

"Please do!"

After a quick moment of silence, Charity said, "I feel terrible about how Mom has spoken to you. Dawson filled me in."

"Thank you, Charity. But you don't owe me an apology."

"I just don't want Dawson to lose you over something our mom said."

Marisa's mind whirled with thoughts that would end this

conversation topic. Her future with Dawson was theirs to figure out.

"Your mom has a right to her own opinion, Charity," she said. "And I know that you and Dawson do not agree with her."

"Absolutely not! I don't want to hold you up, but even if you and Dawson don't work out, promise me that we will still be friends."

"Charity! Of course we will be. My relationship with Dawson is separate from our friendship."

"You're the sister I always wanted, Marisa." Charity sounded as if she was crying but doing her best to hide it.

"I love you, Charity. We are sisters of the heart, and we will be sisters of the heart forever and for always. Okay?"

"Okay."

"Do you believe me?"

"You wouldn't tell me a lie."

"No, I wouldn't."

"That's why I believe you."

They said their fifth *goodbye* as Marisa pulled into the parking lot of the theater. She put the car in park, turned off the engine, and stared at the old brick theater that had become a second home for her. Even though she was excited to get back home, it didn't change the fact that she would miss the Bronco Theater and every one of the artists who helped her pull off a pretty darn good Mistletoe Pageant.

Marisa was about to get out of the car when the phone rang. It was Charity again.

"I almost forgot to tell you!" Dawson's sister said in a rush. "If you see something in the gossip column that looks really bad, I was there and that picture isn't worth a thousand words. That picture is telling a thousand lies."

Chapter Sixteen

Marisa stood on the stage and looked out onto the empty seats. Now that the pressure of putting on a show for Bronco was gone, she felt a deep sense of melancholy. If the mayor of Bronco asked her to put on the next Mistletoe Pageant, Marisa believed she would say "no." She had the right singers, the right musicians and all of the stars had aligned for her *this* time She couldn't imagine seeing Dawson with another woman on his arm, staring at her from the front row with the rest of John family as they watched Charity pull off another triumphant performance. It would be too painful to handle.

"There she is." Agnes walked out onto the stage. "I will miss you, Marisa."

"Thank you, Agnes. For everything." Marisa hugged the older woman. "I wouldn't have been able to put on a puppet show much less a Mistletoe Pageant without you."

"It does my old heart good to know that I could support someone as amazing as you," Agnes said. The older woman was not one for emotion so she turned away, took a moment to collect herself. When she turned back, she had successfully pushed down any sadness and she asked, "So you're all packed up?"

Marisa nodded. "Dawson is meeting me here and after that, I'll drive back to Tenacity."

"And another show."

"Yes. I'm actually exhausted, but I'll be running on adrenaline for the next couple of weeks," she said.

Agnes offered to make her one last pot of high octane coffee for the road; Marisa was grateful for the offer. She had tossed and turned all night thinking about the conversation she would have with Dawson. She intended to end their relationship, in part, to protect each of them from bigger heartbreak down the road.

Marisa followed Agnes to the lounge and while she was waiting on the coffee, she saw the *Bronco Bulletin* on the counter, picked it up and turned to the gossip column. There, she found a picture of Dawson cuddled up with a very pretty blonde, and then a picture of her singing the anthem at the rodeo. The caption read: "Dawson John's Tale of Two Women."

"Trash," Agnes said with disdain.

"Charity warned me about this."

"Junk, plain and simple. I heard this was a setup."

"Are you serious?"

"You know I always am."

Marisa sat down at the table and ran her hand over the photo of Dawson. "If I didn't know better, I would think Dawson was playing around on me."

Agnes poured her the first cup out of the pot.

"Everything I did here with Dawson, I always wondered if there was someone hiding somewhere just waiting to catch us doing something wrong."

"Or making it look like you were." Agnes joined her with a mug of coffee.

"What's the point?"

"To sell newspapers. That's it in a nutshell. Abernathys,

Taylors and Johns sell papers. Build them up, tear them down, cha-ching."

"I won't miss the fishbowl that's for darn sure," Marisa said with a frown.

"No. I suspect not." They finished their last cup of coffee and Agnes hugged her for a long while before she said, "Well, let's get on with it. Can't get anything done if we're blubbering all day."

And that was the last words, for now, from her dear friend Agnes.

Marisa returned to the stage, grateful for the quiet time theater to say goodbye to the theater. While she was sitting on the edge of the stage, with her legs dangling, swinging back and forth, she could look back and imagine the first time she ever laid eyes on Dawson. She remembered her immediate reaction was one of annoyance and disbelief. *Annoyance* because he was being disruptive and *disbelief* that any person could be as downright perfect as Dawson. He had Hollywood bone structure that could rival George Clooney, Brad Pitt and any of the Hemsworth brothers. And, she thought, not for the first time, that he would make very pretty babies.

As if she had conjured him by thinking about him, Dawson walked through the door. He paused, stared at her and then he strode toward the stage in his easy manner, until he reached her, put his hands on her waist and swung her down to her feet. Without one word being spoken, Dawson took her face into his strong, capable hands and kissed her with all of the passion that he no doubt felt for her. It was the same passion that she felt for him and him alone.

"I miss you like no other." Dawson put his forehead against hers. "An hour feels like a week when I'm away from you."

"I…" She paused to consider what she was about to say, not wanting to lead him on. "I miss you too, Dawson."

"You don't have to miss me, *mi amor*!" Dawson caught her gaze and held on to it. "I'm right here. I've always been right here. Waiting for you. I know that now. All of the roads I have traveled were leading me to this moment with you."

Dawson took her by the hand and led her up to the seat where they had fallen in love at first sight.

Still holding her hand, he asked beseechingly, "Please talk to me, Marisa. Tell me what's going on in that brilliant mind of yours. If you meant what you said that you didn't blame me for the horrible ways my parents acted, then why have you pushed me away?"

She looked at their intertwined hands, wanting to say the right words that conveyed the right meaning.

"If your parents can't accept me, Dawson, there isn't any sense in continuing on. It's early yet. We can do the most loving thing and let each other go now before we involve anyone else."

"Like our children."

"Yes," she said. "Like our children. Innocent bystanders."

"And if I don't care what my parents want—"

"They will always be your parents, Dawson. I cannot be a part of you losing them. I couldn't live like that, *knowing* that."

Dawson looked away and he saw resignation in her eyes when he looked back at her. "So there's no way to win."

"Dawson," Marisa said, "I do love you."

"And I love you," he said. "My gut is telling me there is more to this, Marisa. There is something between us—or maybe it's *someone* else?"

He wasn't exactly wrong. Marisa breathed in and then let it out slowly. "I don't know if I can explain it."

"Please try."

She slipped her hand out of his and put both of her hands together in her lap. "Ever since I was a little girl, I always had a picture in my mind of the man I would marry."

Dawson waited with an intense look in his ocean-blue eyes,

"I thought I'd marry a man like my dad. Hardworking, focused on family and community."

"And that's not what you see when you look at me?"

"No."

"Maybe your husband will struggle to make a living…"

"He's a hard worker…"

"Maybe struggles financially," he countered. "And of course he doesn't spend his time rock climbing, skydiving…"

"Gambling…"

Marisa saw a cloud enter Dawson's eyes as he stood up, put his hands into his pockets and paced around a bit before he turned back to her. "So what you're saying—and stop me if I'm wrong—is this whole entire time I've been competing in a head-to-head battle with a fantasy man who only exists in your imagination and I'm *losing*?"

Dawson stood a few feet away from her but he felt a million miles away. His eyes turned stormy blue-gray as they filled with a deep sense of rejection.

"I knew there was something else, but I just couldn't put my finger on it," Dawson told her as much as he was telling himself. "Now it all makes sense. I was always going to lose you, Marisa, wasn't I? How can anyone win against a man who doesn't actually exist?"

She couldn't deny it because what he said was true.

"Let me ask you a question. If I gave all of my money

away to whatever cause you want, could I win against that perfect man in your head? Or am I damaged goods because I was raised by wealthy parents?"

"The money isn't the issue," Marisa tried to explain, "It's about what someone does with the money that matters to me."

"No fun, just give to the community until there's nothing left."

"I'm sorry that I've hurt you, Dawson." Marisa stood up. "I didn't want us to end like this."

Dawson dragged his hands through his hair. "I didn't want us to end *ever*! But you are so damned stubborn, so damned determined to break things off for a figment of your imagination! A ghost! Has it ever occurred to you that you are discriminating against me?"

"Don't be ridiculous." She frowned at him, arms now folded protectively in front of her body.

"You have painted me with a broad brush, Marisa. All people with money are bad…"

"That's not true," she interjected defensively.

"…and all people without money are good. Black and white without any gray area," Dawson said angrily. "I could have met you where you are, Marisa. If you had only let me in! Instead, you're running away!"

"I'm going home, Dawson, not running away," she said. "I want you to answer this. Be honest. Brutally honest."

Dawson had his hands jammed into the front pockets of his jeans, his handsome face wracked with pain she knew that she had put there! And it hurt—it ached—and she just wanted it to stop for both of them.

"Could you live my life in Tenacity? It's a simple life but a good life. I'm a music teacher and a community organizer.

I'm not going to jump out of airplanes or lose thousands of dollars in Vegas even if I had millions in the bank."

Dawson stared at her for several minutes before he said, "So no compromise, Marisa? No negotiation? Just your way or the highway."

Did he have a point? Was she too rigid, too focused on helping others—and doing it her way—that she was unwilling to compromise? And because he had made a point that hit home, she shook her head, trying to think of what to say next and coming to the conclusion that she couldn't find even one good word in her muddled brain.

And that's when Marisa felt like her head was spinning; suddenly she felt hot and sweaty and confused. Dawson crossed the short distance between them, pulled her into his arms, kissed her like a man who would kiss her, hold her and love her for the rest of his life. He buried his face in her neck, holding on to her a while longer while she held on to him.

"I love you, Marisa," Dawson said. "And I know without any doubt that I will love you for the rest of my life."

And then, Dawson turned on his heel and walked away from her, leaving her speechless and frozen in her spot. She waited for it, she watched for it, but Dawson never once looked back.

In the week after Marisa had ended their relationship and had returned to Tenacity, Dawson had avoided his parents and spent time with his brothers rotating their large herds of cattle to different pastures. His brothers didn't expect him to talk, and that suited him just fine. Several women who read the gossip column that had put one small kernel of truth in his breakup with Marisa approached him when he was in town, but he brushed them off as gently as he could. He didn't need another woman; he needed Marisa.

"Hey there, stranger." Charity found him in one of the smaller, less central, horse barns on the Double J.

"Hey, sis."

Charity rested her arms on the stall gate and watched him groom a lovely coal black mare with a long, thick raven mane and tail that he had recently purchased at an auction.

"She's gorgeous."

"Yes, she is."

"What did you name her?"

"La Bella Reina," he said. "The beautiful queen."

Charity didn't say anything about the name; it could remain unspoken. When he had named the new mare, Marisa, as she always was no matter how hard he tried, was in the forefront of his mind.

"Have you spoken to her?" Charity asked.

"Nope." Dawson brushed the mare's neck. "Don't expect to."

"So, that's it?" Charity started to pick at that scab. "Done deal?"

Dawson stopped brushing. "Don't go rewriting history, sis. She broke up with me, not the other way around!"

"I know that." Charity frowned at him with a deep wrinkle between her golden eyebrows. "But you're the man."

He started brushing again. "What are you driving at, Charity?"

"Marisa is a modern woman with some old-fashioned values. She would expect you to fight for her."

"Damn it, Charity! For the last time, she broke up with me! I've made a jackass out of myself trying to get her to accept me as her man and I'm done! I've suffered enough humiliation on that front and I'm not going to do it again."

There was a good long silence between them before Charity said in a less confrontational tone, "You haven't even tried to talk to Mom about Marisa."

"Why in the hell would I?"

"Because you are the only one who can bring Mom over to your side of things. If she changes sides, Dad will too."

"I've never gotten through to her, Charity. Not on the first time and not on time fifty."

"Dawson!" Charity's tone sharpened again. "If you love Marisa as much as you say that you do, you have to try! She doesn't want to lose *you* any more than *you* want to lose her. Have you noticed a common denominator, Dawson?"

"Yeah. I caught it."

After another silence, Charity asked, "Can I tell you something that must be taken to your grave?"

"What's that?"

Charity looked around and then whispered as if ears were everywhere, "I'm the one who sent an anonymous letter to the mayor about Marisa. I hyped up her credentials and suggested hiring her for the pageant."

Dawson stopped his work on the mare to look at her. "So, you're the one Mom has been trying to ferret out? Enemy number one?"

His sister had a very proud expression on her face. "Yep. I'm enemy number one."

Dawson hadn't laughed or smiled since Marisa left town but that made him laugh out loud.

"You're gutsy, baby sis. I'll give you that."

"So, in a way, I'm the one who brought you and Marisa together."

"I'll try not to hold that against you."

"Not my point, actually," Charity said with another frown. "I brought the two of you together, so I must insist that you make amends with Marisa. I want her to be my sister for real, which means that you need to marry her because my other brothers already have wives."

Dawson opened the stall door and joined Charity in the aisle. "We have spoiled you rotten, haven't we?"

"Not sure what your point is…"

"Charity, I'm getting pretty tired of explaining this to you, so this is the last time. She broke up with me. I'm not the man she wants. If you've got a problem with that, talk to Marisa."

"I have. And she misses you. I can hear it in her voice."

Dawson threw the brush into a bucket harder than was needed. "Well, I guess that makes one of us because she hasn't answered my texts or my calls."

"Absence makes the heart grow fonder," Charity said. "She misses you, Dawson. Call her."

"I'll think about it. Okay? But that's it. No more of this."

Charity flung herself into his arms and hugged him tightly. "Thank you, Dawson!"

"I'm not promising anything here," he called after her as she disappeared from view.

Marisa was back in Tenacity and she felt grateful to be back in her tiny two bedroom, one bath brick ranch and her comfy bed snuggling with Saint Nick, the kitten she had rescued from the Tenacity community center. Charity and she were in regular communication, but she was careful not to ask about Dawson and Charity never offered even the smallest glimpse into Dawson's life. They were both trying to navigate an emotional land mine without putting strain on their friendship. It was difficult to admit, but she shouldn't have promised Charity that their relationship would remain the same. How could it?

"All right! Let's start that dance sequence from the beginning! Step ball change, step ball change, stomp, stomp, clap once, clap twice, and then come back to your partner."

Marisa was teaching her Tenacity performers a new dance that she had developed for the Bronco show. Rehearsals for the Tenacity show had been a lifeline for her. When she wasn't at the theater, she spent time with her family and her friends, doing her best to not miss Dawson. But no matter how she tried to fix the gaping hole in her heart left by Dawson, it didn't work. At night, Marisa had plenty of time to mull over the valid points Dawson had made during their last conversation in the Bronco Theater. Perhaps she *was* painting him with a broad brush, judging him too harshly and denying his ability to grow to become her perfect match. After all, wouldn't she also need to grow no matter who she married?

"Beautiful!" Marisa clapped for her dancers. "Let's take a ten minute break."

While the performers moved to the side of the room to rest, Marisa worked through some new steps, eyes closed as she imagined how the movements would coincide with the lyrics of the songs. She took two steps back, spun around, and then once she felt she had worked out the sequence, she looked at herself in the wall of mirrors and then she froze her in her tracks.

"Merry Christmas, Marisa."

There stood Dawson John, in Tenacity, crashing another one of her rehearsals. Dawson was dressed in jet-black jeans, black cowboy boots and a black button-down shirt, tucked in. Instead of a Stetson, Dawson had donned a Santa hat, a thick white beard and carried a sack of presents flung over his shoulder.

"Merry Christmas." She took a step toward him. "I've missed you."

"Missing you has been my constant companion."

"I'm sorry." She took another step.

"I love you, Marisa," Dawson said, and that was met with cheers and whistles and clapping from her performers who were well aware of her breakup with Bronco's infamous Dawson John.

"I love you." Marisa walked toward him as tunnel vision took over and she forgot that anyone was in the room other than the man of her newly formed dreams. All she could see was him, and all she could hear was the rapid beating of her heart.

He met her halfway, as he had always told her that he wanted to do.

"Te amo, mi amor." She told him she loved him in Spanish when she reached him.

"Te amo, mi amor."

Dawson learning bits and pieces of Spanish only endeared him to her more. Knowing that Dawson was her destiny, she rose up onto her tiptoes and kissed him sweetly with a promise for more in a private setting.

"Your beard tickles, Santa." She teased him, her body buzzing with electricity that always happened when her cowboy was nearby.

"I was hoping you couldn't resist a sexy Santa," he said with a wink.

"I can't. And I won't! Not for one more minute!" Marisa said as she turned to her performers. "That's a wrap!"

That started another round of cheers and catcalls as she hooked her arm with Dawson's. "How long are you here for?"

"For as long as it takes," Dawson said, his blue eyes full

of love for her to see so clearly. "I've taken a room at Tenacity Inn. You got to know Bronco, now it's my turn to get to know Tenacity. Any I fully intend to show you that I can be the man of your dreams."

Marisa smiled at that, moving closer to him. "And I'm going to show you that I can live a little and splurge on a trip to Vegas every once in a while."

"Damn I love you."

She laughed happily. "Damn I love you."

Happy to be reunited, arm in arm, Marisa asked him, "Would you like to come home with me? I have a present for you under my Christmas tree."

"Lead the way home, *mi amor.*"

When Charity had suggested that he go to Tenacity dressed as a modern sexy Santa, Dawson had thought she was nuts. But darn it if it hadn't worked. He had just pulled into Marisa's driveway, lined with cheerful candy canes, and the house, the windows, the doors, and all of the trees had been covered with lights. He parked his truck, eager to be alone with the woman he fully intended to marry.

"It's small." Marisa opened the front door. "But it's cozy."

"I like it," he said. "It holds your spirit."

He followed her into the house and was greeted with the scent of pine trees and cinnamon and vanilla that permeated the quaint living room. Marisa took his coat to hang up before she turned to him with a smile. "I kind of miss the beard."

"I'll wear it every Christmas, just for you."

Marisa got them some hot chocolate with marshmallows while he made friends with Saint Nick on her love seat. Then she knelt next to her cheerful, sparkly tree and searched for his present.

"I didn't know if I would have a chance to give this to you." She handed him a small box. "I hope you like it."

Dawson unwrapped the present, took the lid off of the box, and found a heavy, polished silver buckle that featured a lone cowboy on a horse out on the prairie. There was a small mine-cut diamond on the cowboy's neckerchief.

"It was my grandfather's. He was a vaquero. A Mexican cowboy," she told him. "Do you like it?"

"I love it," Dawson said, shocked at the content of the box. "But I can't accept this."

"I want you to have it," she said. "My grandfather, God rest his soul, gave it to me to pass down to my children."

Dawson then realized the magnitude of this gift. "So, let me get this straight...you are giving me this because you see me as your future husband and the father of your children?"

She put her hand on his. "Yes. I can. And... I want to say that I'm sorry for how things between us ended..."

He hugged her tightly and kissed her sweetly. "Let's leave that in the past and focus on the future."

With Marisa's help, he switched out his old buckle for her grandfather's. "How does it look?"

"Like it was meant for you."

He gave her another "thank you" kiss before he pulled a present out of his Santa bag and handed her a box that he had wrapped himself and it was, admittedly, a hot mess.

Marisa unwrapped the box and looked inside. Her eyes widened as she took an etched piece of glass.

"Is this the..."

"Bronco Theater."

"How did you do this, Dawson?"

"I found a place that could turn photographs into glass art," he said with a shrug. "I thought you'd like it."

She gave him a big hug. "I love it!"

Marisa took the glass art over to her mantel and put it in the center as a crown jewel.

"There's more," he said as he pulled the last present out of his Santa bag.

"I don't think anything can top that," she said told him.

"Let's just see about that." He put a small box wrapped beautifully in red sparkly paper topped with an ornate white-and-green-striped bow.

"It's so pretty," Marisa said.

She opened the box to find a necklace with a dainty piano charm. It was simple, unadorned and completely spoke to her heart.

"It's perfect," Marisa said before she kissed him. "Will you put it on me?"

"My pleasure."

Marisa lifted up her hair while Dawson brought the necklace around her neck and clasped it.

He then took the opportunity to kiss her, slow, long, with a promise of more.

"How does it look?"

"You make it beautiful."

The expression on Marisa's pretty face confirmed that he had bought the right gifts for his beloved.

"We were both thinking about each other," Marisa said, touching the charm on her neck. "We were both wishing for a Christmas miracle."

They embraced, holding on to each other, knowing that they had found their forever person. Marisa would be his only love, the mother of his children and the keeper of his heart. After some time holding Marisa tight in his arms, he said, "I want to tell you something, Marisa."

She waited, but her body tensed as she felt a shift in his tone to the more serious.

"My mother would like to come to Tenacity for lunch. She wants to spend time with you. To get to know you."

Marisa pushed herself up to look in his face and waited.

"She understands how much you mean to me, Marisa. How much I love you," he said, "and that I fully intend to marry you."

Marisa's eyes teared up as she reached for his hand. "I love you."

"She wants to make amends. Can you give her a chance?"

"Yes." She nodded. "If she is sincere, I can."

As the pain of weeks apart dissipated, Marisa went to the kitchen, with a promise for a speedy return, to get them some spiked eggnog. When she came back, Dawson was standing in her living room holding a sprig of mistletoe over his head.

"So, do you still believe in the magic of mistletoe?" he asked.

Marisa put down the mugs and stepped into his arms. "More now than I ever have in my life."

After three kisses beneath the mistletoe, Dawson took out his phone and snapped a selfie to capture the moment.

"We make a handsome couple," he told her, "do I have your permission to post this?"

Marisa laughed. "Feel free to post to any social media you please."

He touched a few buttons on his phone and then showed her. "Are you going to change your status to in a relationship?"

"Yes. Of course I will." His future wife hugged him tightly. "Will you?"

"Already did it," he said. "Just waiting on you to catch up."

Dawson gave his true love another Christmas kiss beneath the mistletoe. He kissed Marisa with all of the love in his heart and he knew without any doubt that theirs would be a lifetime of love and romance and children. And he would make darn sure that every doorway in their house would hold a sprig of mistletoe, no matter the time of year.

* * * * *

Look for the next installment in the new continuity
Montana Mavericks: The Trail to Tenacity

The Maverick's Christmas Countdown
by Heatherly Bell

On sale December 2024
Wherever Harlequin books and ebooks are sold.

And don't miss the previous books,
Redeeming the Maverick
by New York Times *bestselling author Christine Rimmer*

The Maverick Makes the Grade
by USA TODAY *bestselling author Stella Bagwell*

That Maverick of Mine
by Kathy Douglass

Available now!